PERCEPTION

Published by Lue Cleveland
PO Box 12351
Albany, New York 12212

Copyright 2014

Publication Date: October 2014
ISBN 978-0-578-15227-1

Printed in the United States of America

Acknowledgements

Writing a book requires a considerable amount of energy and determination. Therefore first and foremost, I thank God for the ability and foresight to pursue this vision. I would like to thank my husband for his support and encouragement. I thank him for not just standing by me but believing that I could pursue this dream and for his insistence that the book was good. I would also like to thank my three sons and my sister for their continual support and positive feedback during this journey. Thanks to my son, Nathan and Brian Burnett for an amazing cover. I absolutely love it.

I really can't thank Ms. McCartan enough for editing my work. I consider myself fortunate to have found a professional with the combination of skills and passion that she possesses. Her competency afforded me the opportunity to completely focus on the story and I am very grateful for her assistance.

Much gratitude and appreciation to all those who provided encouraging words, well wishes and helped to make this book a reality.

Dedication

This book is dedicated to the loving memory of my parents who planted the everlasting seeds of responsibility and strong work ethics and to my ancestors, including those whose life memoirs I will never know but upon whose accomplishments I stand.

Chapter 1

Brooklin's eyes open as an arm moves around her waist. She wonders if morning has arrived. She is so tired. She turns and gazes at her husband's face, noticing the bags under his eyes and his graying hair. He smiles and moves closer to her. He is such a handsome man. He kisses her and his arms tighten around her.

Traffic is heavy. It's nearly eight o'clock and Brooklin's late. Fatigue, rushing and satisfying everyone is quickly becoming her reality. As she drives during the morning rush hour, Brooklin convinces herself that the choices she has made in life are good ones. Over a year ago, she left her former job, resigning after seven years. She just couldn't return to that office, that building. She just couldn't. Her hands begin to sweat. "Okay, Brooklin, don't think about it, put it behind you," she says to herself as she realizes she has arrived at work. She locks her car and walks toward the hotel.

Brooklin admires Logan Courtyard's elegant exterior design, the blooming shrubs and plants lining the curving drive and walkway, the sound of splashing water from a magnificent central fountain and intoxicating fragrances from a multitude of radiant flowers. Beyond the front door lies a spectacular spacious lobby with recessed ceiling and chandeliers creating an unforgettable place of grandeur. Sunlight streams through ceiling to floor windows, providing a breath-taking view, a panorama of the harbor and earth tone furnishings add a level of sophistication. A suspended fireplace, the "Jewel of the Lobby," dominates the rear of the reception area and features a clear glass panel that can be viewed from all sides.

Jamie, a young desk clerk who has worked for the hotel for over a year, says a cheerful "Good morning, Brooklin." Brooklin smiles, returns the greeting and walks quickly past the front desk through the double doors to her office. She unlocks her office door and walks to her large mahogany desk. A few minutes later Taylor, the hotel's assistant general manager, arrives to brief Brooklin on the problems from last evening and on-going hotel activities. Taylor, who has worked for the hotel for five years, is an attractive thirty-two year old single woman.

She doesn't seem to have a life outside of the hotel. Brooklin listens to her, provides strategies and tells her she'll join her in the staff meeting in thirty minutes.

As Taylor walks out of the office, Brooklin checks her phone messages. There is a message from Luke, her 21 year old son. Both Luke and her daughter Laila who is 20 attend the local college, work part-time in the family's business and share an apartment. Brooklin returns Luke's call who, of course, doesn't answer. She leaves a message. There is also a message from her brother Jim, and she reflects a moment before returning his call.

Brooklin inherited the hotel from her mother, who died suddenly about a year before and Jim has not been able to accept this fact. Their mother supported Jim financially for most of his adult life. Over the years, this financial help created a dependency. When their mother died, Jim turned to Brooklin for the monetary support he'd received from their mother. While Brooklin understood her mother's good intent, she would not be a crutch for Jim. She gave him a job at the hotel and told him he had to work for his salary. Jim felt betrayed by his mother and Brooklin. This had a significant impact on their relationship. His personality was negative, his productivity at work was low and he resented Brooklin. However, she would not allow Jim's negativity to interfere with her primary goals for Logan Courtyard nor would she encourage Jim's unpleasant behavior. Brooklin telephones Jim who answers sounding winded. "Jim, it's Brooklin returning your call."

"Brooklin, I will not be at work for the remainder of the week," Jim abruptly says.

"What is the problem?" Brooklin asks. No response. "Jim, you were absent from work two days last week and now you're telling me you will not be at work for the remainder of this week? Jim, this can't continue. When you arrive at the hotel on Monday, talk to my secretary Erica regarding a time for you and me to meet. I know I have a couple of meetings Monday morning, but I need to talk to you as soon as my meetings are over. And Jim, I don't want to have to look for you Monday. We definitely need to talk."

Jim sighs, "Okay, Brooklin, I'll see you on Monday."

Brooklin quickly disconnects from Jim and buzzes Erica telling her to schedule some time for her to meet with Jim on Monday. Jim has not been the best brother. However, Brooklin has taken the high road realizing his conduct is not a result of anything she has done nor does it originate from any of her actions. She provided him with a job where he could earn a decent income instead of always asking for a handout. Brooklin has chosen not to engage in Jim's cynicisms except when his conduct affects Logan Courtyard. Business is business. Jim needs to return to the source of his problems: himself.

Brooklin begins her morning walk through the hotel. She loves this hotel with its twelve floors, luxurious rooms and suites, state of the art spa and fitness center, swimming pools and whirlpools. Logan Courtyard offers a stylish boutique, gift shop, valet parking, hair salon as well as dry cleaning and laundry service. The hotel is one of the city's best venues for gatherings with its two impressive banquet rooms, five meeting rooms, and 24-hour business center with advanced technology. Its superb restaurant creates delicious cuisines with fireside tables, stunning beach and harbor views while the bar has a dance floor and private entrance. Logan Courtyard extends to its guests unparalleled luxury accommodations, the perfect getaway.

Larry, one of the security guards, approaches Brooklin as she returns to her office. "Brooklin, can I speak to you for a few minutes?"

"Larry, I'm about to go into a meeting. Is there a problem with security?"

"No," he answers. "It doesn't concern hotel security."

"In that case, Larry, I can meet with you around 11:30."

"Ok, Brooklin, but it's important," Larry whispers. Brooklin looks at him with a little uncertainty, hesitates, and then walks into her office to obtain her iPad.

"Okay, Larry, I'll see you at 11:30." She closes her office door and walks toward Meeting Room Two. Brooklin enters the meeting and moves toward the head of the table. The spacious meeting rooms have lavish furnishings and state of the art conference technology. In all, there are ten staff in attendance, representing all hotel departments and services.

Each staff member provides updates regarding their department while her secretary Erica records the minutes. Toward the end of the meeting, Brooklin directs a question to marketing. "Karen, before we leave, I'd like more information regarding online promotions and details concerning our guests for the Teen Center's phonathon. Also, please schedule a time with Erica for you and me to meet with our two tenants." Logan Courtyard rents space to a dry cleaning facility and hair salon. Brooklin likes to show management's concern by having occasional meetings with the tenants. There is a knock on the door and Jamie informs Brooklin that her son Luke is on the phone. Brooklin returns to her office and retrieves the call. "Hello, Luke."

"Hi, Mom, I've been trying to reach you. I'm at the hospital. I hurt my ankle playing basketball. I think it might be broken."

"What? Are you at Memorial?" she asks.

"Yes," he says groaning a little.

"Okay, I should be there in about

twenty minutes." Brooklin tells her secretary she's leaving for the day and to call her if there are any problems.

In the hospital's emergency room, Brooklin gives her name to a young, red haired nurse and asks for her son's location. The nurse checks the computer and gives Brooklin Luke's room number and directions. Brooklin walks down to the end of the hall and makes a left. Luke's room is the third room on the right. Brooklin finds Luke lying on the bed, staring at the ceiling. She focuses her attention on his swollen ankle and foot. "How are you doing? Are you in a lot of pain?" she asks.

"It's uncomfortable but I'm okay, Mom. I called your cell phone and your office. Were you in a meeting all morning?" he asks.

Brooklin checks her cell phone and sees a missed call from Luke. "Sorry, my cell phone was on vibrate. How long have you been at Memorial? Who brought you here?" she asks. Luke tells her he has been at the hospital about an hour. His friend Lamar brought him but had to leave to pick up his girlfriend. "Luke, what happened?" she asks.

"Lamar and I walked down to the campus gym for a quick workout. We didn't have class until the afternoon. There were a few guys in the gym shooting around and we decided to play a little pick-up basketball. I went up for a lay-up and came down on one of the player's foot and twisted my ankle," he explains.

Brooklin thinks to herself, "All this for a pick-up basketball game?" Luke informs her that he had not gone for x-rays yet. Brooklin settles herself in the chair, checks her phone again and begins to compose a checklist of hotel business while Luke focuses on the television.

Minutes later, Luke and Brooklin hear a woman's voice in the next room.

"Oh my God, Josh, what happened to you?"

A male voice responds, "I don't want to talk about it."

"You don't want to talk about it? I want to know what happened to you!"

Luke and Brooklin look at each other curiously. Then they hear a nurse say, "We are going to take Josh to x-ray now."

A few minutes pass and they hear two

women talking. "Do you know what happened to Josh?"

"Rumor has it that Josh borrowed money and unfortunately didn't make the payments, resulting in Big Mel attacking him with a baseball bat."

"A baseball bat? Are you serious? Someone named Big Mel did this to Josh, breaking his arm, fracturing ribs and slashing his face? What kind of animal would do that?"

"Well, that's what loan sharks do," the lady says.

"Loan shark? Did anyone call the police?"

"I think the hospital reported Josh's injuries to the police. Josh said the police were here earlier to question him. Apparently, he didn't tell them anything. Before you arrived, Josh muttered something about how he wasn't going to let the police get him killed."

"I wonder how much money Josh owes this Big Mel. I can't believe this. How could he allow himself to get into this type of predicament? Do you know why Josh borrowed the money? Was it a gambling debt?"

"I don't know why Josh needed to borrow money. This entire situation is outrageous."

"What was Josh thinking?"

"Apparently, Josh wasn't thinking."

Luke looks at his mother and mouths "wow."

Brooklin says to Luke, "That's why you don't get involved with those criminal types."

"Well, Mom, I can't make any promises." Brooklin gazes at Luke. Luke looks at her laughing, "Mom, I'm joking. I'm just joking."

"Well apparently, you're not in that much pain if you're able to tell humorless jokes."

Brooklin arrives at work early the next day to find Erica waiting for her at her office door. Nervously Erica says she has urgent news. Once inside, she blurts out, "Brooklin, last night Larry was hit by a car outside of his home. It was a hit and run. He's in a coma and in critical condition."

Brooklin gasps, "What?" She immediately thinks back to yesterday when

Larry stopped her in the hall and asked to talk with her. She wonders what he wanted to tell her. He had said it was important. Now, he's in a coma? She recalls what she knows about Larry. He's in his late 40s, divorced and lives alone in a small house about twenty minutes from the hotel. He has a son from his marriage. She asks Erica if she has any more information about what happened.

"No," she says.

"What hospital is he in?" asks Brooklin.

"Memorial," Erica replies.

Brooklin turns and stares out the window for a moment, seeing yet not seeing two sailboats as they slowly drift by. "Do I have any meetings scheduled for this morning?"

"No," Erica responds. "Your first meeting is at 1pm with Karen from marketing and sales, Ted from dry cleaning and Laura from the hair salon."

"Erica, please call Carl and tell him I need to see him."

About ten minutes later, Carl, head of security and valet parking, enters her office. "Good morning, Brooklin. I guess you've heard about Larry."

"I did. What do you know about this hit and run?"

"Not much. I'm told that Larry was getting out of his car near his home when a vehicle hit him and fled the scene. I will check Larry's time card for the time he left the hotel yesterday. But I don't know any more than that."

"If you learn more, please inform me and, Carl, we need to assign someone to first shift security as soon as possible."

"Will do," Carl says as he leaves her office.

Brooklin informs Erica she's on her way to Memorial and asks Erica to contact her on her cell if needed. Once in the car, Brooklin looks for a cd, one that will help her calm her nerves. So much has happened in the last couple of days. She takes a deep breath, swallows and selects one of Ruben's cds. She listens to that R&B singer and begins to exhale. She absolutely loves his smooth, velvety voice. "Thanks, Ruben, for the momentary haven," she says to herself.

Chapter 2

Brooklin walks to the front door of Memorial Hospital. She was just here yesterday with Luke in the ER until late afternoon. However, today she's entering through the front of the hospital. As she reaches for the door, she admires the landscaping. Yesterday, she didn't even notice. Brooklin makes a mental note to try to stay in the moment. She is always in deep thought and not taking in her surroundings. She enters the hospital and walks to the reception desk.

"Good morning! I'm here to see Larry Carter." The receptionist checks her computer.

"Mr. Carter is in the Trauma ICU on the fourth floor. Are you family?" she asks.

"No, I'm a friend," Brooklin replies. The receptionist explains that Brooklin will not be able to visit Larry; however, she directs her to the 4th floor Trauma ICU waiting room. Brooklin follows her direction. She gazes in the waiting room and sees a middle-aged man sitting in a chair staring at the television. She walks inside; the man looks up briefly and then looks down disappointedly.   Brooklin walks over, introduces herself and asks if he's Larry's brother, Mark. Larry had spoken of his older brother Mark, stating they were close and they were the only family remaining.

"Oh, Brooklin, Larry always speaks highly of you." His face warms a little as he talks to her.

"May I ask what the doctors have told you about Larry's condition?" she asks with concern.

"The doctors told me Larry was found unconscious and remains unresponsive. He suffered facial fractures -- broken cheek bones, broken nose and a broken jaw. He also has a broken leg, broken ribs, ruptured bladder and a punctured lung. Right now, I'm hoping Larry will be strong enough to make it through surgery. He sustained a lot of injuries," Mark says. He looks at her with anguish on his face, "The doctor asked if Larry had a Living Will or if he had a Healthcare Proxy. I can't believe someone did this to him."

Brooklin tells him how sorry she is that this happened to Larry. "Have the police talked to you?" she asks.

"They were here questioning me and providing information about an hour ago. Larry's ex-wife and son stopped by before the police arrived. They told me they had been questioned earlier this morning. I'm relieved law enforcement is already working the case. They informed me a man driving on Bauknight Ferry saw Larry lying in the road and called 911. The driver also remembered a dark blue Mazda speeding past his car minutes before he saw Larry lying in the street. He believed this might have been the vehicle responsible for striking Larry. The witness said it was dark, he couldn't give any more details about the car and he didn't see the driver. The police believe the witness drove by minutes after Larry was hit, probably saving Larry's life."

They were quiet for a few minutes. "Mark, have you eaten? Can I get you anything?" Brooklin asks.

"No, I'm fine. I can't eat right now," he whispers.

She sat with him making trivial conversations. Max, the second shift security officer, walks in wearing his black security uniform and the two men embrace. Brooklin says her good-byes and asks Mark to please keep her informed on Larry's condition.

Brooklin returns to her car and checks her phone. No messages. She calls Luke on her car's Bluetooth. Luke is at home for a few days after x-rays confirmed he only suffered a sprained ankle. She talks to her son briefly trying not to think about what had occurred with Larry. Luke seems fine. Maggie, the part-time housekeeper, is taking good care of him. She asked Maggie to work full-time this week to help care for Luke. Brooklin's work hours are long and she is grateful to have Maggie. A couple Brooklin and her husband knew for years relocated to Richmond, VA and recommended Maggie to them. She had worked for the couple about four years. The timing was perfect and Maggie came to work for the Covingtons.

Back at the office, Brooklin buzzes Erica. She asks her to send a large flower arrangement to Larry at Memorial and have someone from the hotel restaurant take Mark a hot lunch with coffee and take him dinner as well. About ten minutes later, Erica suddenly bursts into Brooklin's office, grabs the TV remote, turns the television on and stands next to Brooklin as they stare intensely at the news report.

"Good morning, there has been another tragic accident on Bauknight Ferry Road. Larry Carter was hit by a car and found unconscious on the upper part of Bauknight Ferry Road last night, city police report this morning. The victim was getting out of his car when a car struck him and then drove away. Mr. Carter was transported to Memorial Hospital and remains in critical condition. Authorities say the vehicle probably has front-end damage and is missing an outside mirror. Anyone with information relative to the case is asked to call Detective Ryan at (877) 628-2527. This is Carolyn Lark reporting from the south end," says the female brunette reporter.

Erica turns the television off, looks at Brooklin and asks, "What happened at the hospital?"

Brooklin tells Erica about her visit to the hospital and cautions that their conversation must be kept confidential. "Does the staff have any additional information about this accident?" Brooklin asks.

Erica takes a deep breath and says, "Max told a few people that he heard the hit was planned. Someone intentionally hit Larry."

Brooklin can feel her pulse racing and feels slightly light-headed. "Does Max know who hit Larry? Where is he getting this information from?"

Erica says, "I don't know. I'm not sure if Max is telling the truth or just talking. I can't think of anyone who would want to hurt Larry. Larry and Carmen, his ex-wife, have been divorced for two years and I heard they are on amicable terms, although I'm told Carmen is an alcoholic. Larry has a son, Ron, from the marriage. Larry evidently loves and adores his son," Erica says.

"Well, if you hear anything more, please tell me. Will you have Jerry bring me a turkey sandwich with some fruit on the side and a bottle of water? I'm going to try to eat before my meeting with Karen, Ted and Laura." Brooklin says.

"Brooklin, the restaurant has mouthwatering dishes. Why do you constantly order a boring sandwich and a salad?"

Brooklin smiles and says, "Erica, every now and then, I do have one of those mouthwatering delicious dishes. Typically, I try to eat light, just enough to recharge."

"Recharge? If I ate like you, I'd require resuscitation. I would need new life to be breathed into my body." Brooklin looks at Erica, shakes her head and they both laugh. "Seriously, Brooklin, do you ever crave for something like a burger?"

"Erica, I'm always on the move and food is more often than not, secondary. I love good food; however, my waistline reminds me that food is not my friend. And, listen to you. I've noticed you have lost a few pounds."

Erica is quiet a moment and then says, "A turkey sandwich coming up, Mrs. Covington," and returns to her desk.

Brooklin listens to her voice mail and as she puts the phone down, Jerry enters with her lunch. She chooses jazz from her phone apps and the music plays softly as she begins her lunch. She consumes her last strawberry and walks to her desk as her phone rings. The ring tone signals Erica is calling. "Yes, Erica," she says.

"Karen, Ted and Laura are here to meet

with you and Jerry is here to pick up your tray from lunch. Do you need me to come in and take notes?"

"No, if you can finish typing that report for me. Thanks, Erica," Brooklin says.

Jerry removes the tray as Karen, Ted and Laura takes their seats at the conference table. "What happened to Larry is appalling," comments Karen. Ted and Laura agree.

"It is shocking. Hopefully Larry will recover quickly and the responsible party is found," Brooklin says. She transitions the conversation to hotel issues and asks, "Ted, how is everything in dry cleaning?"

"Everything is running pretty smoothly except that, it seems our arrangement with the housekeeping staff is not always being followed," Ted narrows his eyes.

"Can you explain?" Brooklin asks.

Ted continues, "Guests will not always call dry cleaning if they need their clothes cleaned. Instead, they may telephone laundry or the front desk and ask for their clothing to be picked up for dry cleaning. Laundry or the front desk will call dry cleaning immediately and our staff will pick-up the items. If a guest stops housekeeping and asks to have an article of clothing cleaned, dry cleaning may not receive the clothing for a couple of hours and sometimes not until the end of the housekeeping shift. My staff is then forced to clean the items quickly in order for guests to receive their clothing in a timely manner."

Laura agrees that the hair salon is having the same problem. "Everything runs efficiently except when housekeeping is involved," Laura shrugs and almost looks apologetic.

Brooklin makes a note of this. "Have you discussed this with Linda?" Brooklin asks. Both Ted and Laura say they had discussed this with Linda, but the problem still exists. "I actually talked to Taylor about it on Friday," says Ted.

"And has the matter been rectified?" Brooklin asks.

Ted mutters, "It happened again on Monday. However, Brooklin, guests are not aware of the problem because they are receiving their dry cleaning in a timely fashion. Nevertheless, this is beginning to be costly for dry cleaning because we have to perform extra laundry runs."

"Okay, it will be taken care of today," Brooklin says. "Is there anything else?" she asks Ted and Laura. They both nod "no." She reminds them the services they provide to guests are exceptional and that guest online surveys always rate their services as excellent. She thanks them and adjourns the meeting.

Karen updates Brooklin on current promotions. They discuss upcoming parties and accommodations for the special guests working the phonathon this weekend. Brooklin recommends that an employee be assigned to each phonathon guest to be certain all of their needs are met. Additionally, Brooklin tells Karen to ask Erica to schedule a second meeting with her early next week regarding the holiday campaign and to include Luke and Taylor. As Karen stands to leave, she asks how Luke is doing.

Brooklin tells her, "Luke's fine. He just sprained his ankle." As Karen exits, Brooklin calls Erica and asks her to have Linda and Taylor come to her office immediately. They arrive a few minutes later and Brooklin motions for them to sit at the conference table. Brooklin can tell by their expressions that they are aware she is displeased. "I just had a meeting with Ted and Laura and I'm told they're having problems with housekeeping. Can either of you explain why this is occurring?" she asks. Taylor speaks first saying she was told of the situation late Friday afternoon. She had been unable to talk to Linda until Monday because Linda had left for the day on Friday. Monday morning, she discussed this with Linda and was told the problem had been traced to two maids. Linda had talked to them and was certain this would not happen again.

"Who are the two maids?" Brooklin asks.

"Mary and Joan," Linda answers.

"How long have they worked for the hotel?" asks Brooklin.

"I actually hired them at the same time, about six months ago," Linda says.

"Did they complete all parts of the housekeeping training?"

"Yes," Linda answers.

"What type of employees are they?" Brooklin asks.

"They are pretty good," she replies glancing at Taylor.

"Have they missed any days or been

late?" asks Brooklin.

"They both have missed about two days and been late a couple of times," Linda says.

"Okay, well they have left for the day," begins Brooklin. "Tomorrow morning, I want you to meet with the housekeeping staff and be clear in regards to all of their specific responsibilities. Allow Mary and Joan to work their normal schedule and at the end of their shift at 2pm direct Max to bring them in your office, Linda, where you will then terminate their employment. Max should escort them to their lockers to secure their personal belongings and then out of the hotel. Linda, come to my office around noon to obtain their final pay check. I will tell Meghan in accounting and give her the payment information for her records," Brooklin says with a little elevated tone.

"Now, Linda I am a little confused why you would think an employee who has missed two days and been late two days within a six month period is 'a pretty good employee.'" Linda looks embarrassed. "Taylor, I would like you to create a Logan Courtyard DVD that includes a mission statement, guidelines and attendance policy. When completed, please submit it for my approval. I'll have Erica to distribute it to all staff. Thereafter, this DVD should be included in the orientation process. Taylor, I would like you to then make certain that Logan Courtyard policies are followed to the letter.

Linda, I would like you to provide me with an update after you meet with Mary and Joan tomorrow. Ladies, I don't want this to happen again and please do not discuss this with anyone. Only the three of us should be aware of Mary and Joan's dismissal. I do not want them or any other employee to learn of this until Linda tells them in her office at 2:00. Are we clear on this?" They both shake their heads. "Taylor, I would like you to call Max and have him report to Linda's office around 1:45 tomorrow. Make him aware of the situation at that time. Also, Taylor, I would like you to stay a few more minutes."

Linda apologizes once more and leaves the office. "Taylor, why didn't you inform me of this problem?" Brooklin asks.

"Well, I thought I had taken care of it and didn't want to bother you with it," she says.

"Taylor, you gave me an update this

week. This should have been included in the update. I want to know everything regarding this hotel. It doesn't matter how small. I want to make certain you understand this. I don't want to have this conversation again. Is there anything concerning Logan Courtyard that I am not aware of at this time?" Brooklin hesitates. "If so, I want to know right now."

"No," she says, speaking in a low tone.

`"Remember *everything*, Taylor," Brooklin says looking directly in her eyes.

"I understand. I will make certain I inform you of everything. And I will start working on the guidelines and attendance policy as soon as I return to my office," she says as she leaves the room. Brooklin phones Erica and tell her she wants to meet once a month with each department supervisor. Erica asks if Brooklin would like Taylor or any other staff to be included in the meeting. Brooklin tells her no, just the department supervisor and herself. Brooklin thinks, "It is obvious I have to become more involved in the day-to-day operation of the hotel."

Brooklin looks at her in-box. She picks up the folder on top telling herself that she is going to make the most of the next few hours working on this paperwork. Tomorrow morning, she will start on the reports. Work is the best way to channel this negative energy right now.

Once in the privacy of her own office, Taylor throws her iPad on the desk, ranting to herself, "I can't believe Brooklin spoke to me that way. Yeah, I know she has a lot of responsibilities. I managed this hotel when her mother was alive. I oversaw all aspects of the hotel while Brooklin was in her so called 'profession' and working at the hotel part-time. I have sacrificed and given myself to this hotel." She flops down in her chair and places her hands over her face. She looks up and says, "Brooklin needs to bench her ego. Or I will have to bench it for her."

Thirty minutes later, Brooklin's office phone rings. She recognizes Erica's ring tone. "Yes, Erica."

"A Detective Ryan is here to see you, Brooklin. He says he would like to talk to you regarding Larry," Erica says.

Brooklin looks up from her computer and says, "Okay, ask him to come in." The door opens and a tall, handsome medium-built man walks in. He's dressed in a pair of jeans, white shirt and a sports jacket. He has closely cut salt and pepper hair and looks to be about 45. He walks to Brooklin's desk, extends his hand and introduces himself. She extends her hand and smiles politely. He holds her hand a bit longer than necessary; she recovers quickly and withdraws her hand. He stares at her and she realizes her hair is probably a bit untidy. She remembers running her hand through her hair as she worked on the computer. Well at this point, she resists trying to smooth or rub her hand through her hair. He would think she was trying to impress him. She sits down and motions him to have a seat.

Chapter 3

"Good afternoon, Ms. Logan. I'm Detective Ryan. I'm investigating Mr. Carter's case, the hit and run. I understand that he is an employee here at Logan Courtyard."

"It's Mrs. Covington and, yes, Detective Ryan, Mr. Carter is a security guard here at Logan Courtyard."

"Ms. Covington, how long has Mr. Carter worked for Logan Courtyard?"

"He's been an employee for about two years."

"What type of employee is Mr. Carter?" he asks.

"He's a good employee, his attendance is excellent, he's punctual, friendly and a very good security officer."

"How does he get along with the other employees? Does he have friends here at work?"

"I think he relates well with his co-workers. I'm not aware of any specific friendships. However, as I mentioned earlier, he is friendly and pleasant."

"Are you aware of any problems or

conflicts he may have had with another employee or anyone else?"

"No, I'm not, Detective Ryan."

"Have any of the employees discussed with you the circumstances of what happened to Mr. Carter or anything they have heard in regards to the hit and run?"

"I have only heard in passing that employees are stunned and upset. We are all trying to understand how this could have happened to Mr. Carter."

"Ms. Covington, do you know if Mr. Carter was dating anyone or if he was in a relationship?"

"No, I do not know if Mr. Carter was dating anyone or if he was in a relationship." Brooklin hesitates and then continues. "Detective Ryan, I'm assuming from your line of questioning that you may suspect the hit and run was not accidental?"

He chooses his words carefully, "I'm just gathering information, Ms. Covington." He glances at his notes and says, "Would it be all right for me to talk to each of the staff members here at Logan Courtyard?"

"Yes, that will be fine. When would you like to begin, Detective Ryan?"

"Tomorrow morning, as early as possible," he says.

"Okay, I will tell my secretary Erica to print a schedule for you to meet with each staff member in a conference room tomorrow morning beginning at 7am. Would it be acceptable to you to schedule them at thirty minute intervals?"

"That will be fine. I guess I will see you tomorrow," he says gazing at Brooklin. She does not comment. He stands and reaches for her hand again. She extends her hand and just as quickly removes it from his grasp. "It was very nice to meet you, Ms. Covington. You have a first-rate hotel here." He looks at her with a smile, "I have been a guest here a few times."

Brooklin says simply, "Thank you and I hope you enjoyed your stay at Logan Courtyard."

"Yes, I did. The hotel, staff and grounds are superb." He walks to the door and says, "Oh, one last question. Where were you last evening around 10:30 pm?"

She raises an eyebrow and says, "I was home with my husband and son. And if necessary, my family can corroborate my whereabouts."

"It's my job to ask," he says smiling.

"Goodbye, Detective Ryan."

Before Brooklin could call, Erica walks in Brooklin's office and comments, "He is absolutely gorgeous."

Ignoring the comment, Brooklin says, "Erica, please schedule each of our employees to meet with Detective Ryan tomorrow in an available conference room. Schedule them thirty minutes apart, with the housekeeping staff being questioned first because their day ends before the other employees. Also, tell Kevin to provide a continental breakfast, lunch, healthy snacks, coffee and water in the conference room for Detective Ryan. Okay now, I'm going to get some work done. Don't interrupt me unless it's an emergency," Brooklin says as she looks down at the paperwork awaiting her. Erica understands that their talk has ended and exits with her iPad.

At home around 7:30pm, Brooklin finds her husband Colin and Luke sitting in the family room watching sports. What a beautiful site, Brooklin thinks. Luke is still recuperating at home instead of his apartment while his ankle heals. The timing is perfect since Laila's friend, Julie, is spending a couple weeks with Laila until her apartment is ready. "Hello, family," Brooklin says.

They both chime in, "Hi, hello."

"So how are you feeling, Luke?" Brooklin asks as she walks over and gives Colin a quick kiss. She flops down on the couch between Colin and Luke.

"I feel fine, Mom. I'm just a little bored. I'll be glad to return to school in a couple of days."

"I guess you're fine if you're bored," Brooklin says. Colin pours her a glass of wine and returns to sit beside her on the couch. Brooklin places her feet on her husband's thighs and he begins to massage her feet. "Oh, that feels so good!"

"So how was work?" Colin asks. Brooklin tells him about Larry and how she was questioned by Detective Ryan.

"How was your day?" Brooklin asks Colin. He updates her on the Teen Center. About two years ago, Colin and Brooklin bought this run down building on a few acres of land. Her family and a contractor renovated the building and turned it into a Teen Center. As she lays her head back on the couch, Brooklin tells Colin that she will be at the Teen Center Friday morning. The massage feels so good and she quickly falls asleep. Colin wakes her, takes her hand and leads her upstairs to bed.

The next morning, Brooklin is downstairs in the kitchen making turkey bacon, eggs and cheese croissants when Maggie walks in with a big smile. She places the morning newspaper in the chair saying, "Good morning." The morning sun and fresh air rush through the screen door and fill the room. Brooklin smiles warmly and says, "Morning, Maggie, how was your evening?"

"It was nice. Watched television with Joe and fell asleep on the couch," Maggie says laughing.

"Sounds familiar," Brooklin says laughing too.

Colin comes downstairs and they watch the morning news, commenting on the news stories while eating breakfast. As Brooklin is leaving for work, Colin's about to get dressed. He retired last year and is currently managing the Teen Center. "See you tonight," Brooklin says. He reaches over, places a kiss on her lips and winks at her. She smiles and starts out for work.

Brooklin's head is buried in reports when Erica walks into her office. Brooklin had completed her paperwork last night and hopes to complete two reports today. "Good morning, Brooklin." She can tell from Erica's voice and demeanor that she is ready to gossip. "I want to let you know, Taylor was a little annoyed that she was not informed about Detective Ryan interviewing staff members."

"I forgot to tell her," Brooklin says.

"I know," replies Erica. "I forgot too. I called her this morning to inform her, but she seemed a little irritated. Just wanted you to know!"

"Thanks, Erica. But, it really doesn't matter. Has Detective Ryan begun interviewing staff?"

"Yes, he started the interviews at 7am. I came in at 6:30am to make certain everything was set up for him in the conference room. Kevin had the continental breakfast, coffee and bottled water set up for Detective Ryan at 6:40am. Everyone is here today, so things are proceeding smoothly."

"Good, now I need to focus on these reports."

Erica continued, "The women are mesmerized by Detective Ryan. They can't wait to be questioned. You know he's single. I'm told he has been divorced about three years," she says.

Brooklin looks up at her and points to the papers on her desk, "The reports, Erica."

She blushes slightly, "Oh okay, I'll just return to my desk."

Brooklin finishes the reports at 12:30 and asks Erica to tell Jerry to bring her today's newspaper and a Caesar salad with grilled chicken strips, fruit and bottled water. "Okay, one healthy lunch coming up," Erica replies and they both smile as Erica exits.

Jerry arrives with Brooklin's lunch and the newspaper. He pauses a moment and then says, "I have an appointment to talk to that detective who is investigating the hit on Larry."

Brooklin looks up and questions, "The hit?"

He appears nervous and corrects himself, "I mean the hit and run."

"What do you know about the hit and

run, Jerry?" Brooklin asks.

"Nothing, I don't know nothing 'bout it, Ms. Brooklin. That's why I don't know why I have to talk to that detective."

"Jerry, if you don't know anything, you don't have anything to worry about. Just answer the detective's questions. And Jerry, you are not being singled out. Everyone at the hotel is talking to him. He even questioned me." He grumbles, says okay and walks out the door. Brooklin's mouth is a little dry and she drinks some of her bottled water. She re-visits the conversation she just had with Jerry thinking that something was very weird.

Brooklin takes her daily walk through the hotel starting in the lobby where she finds Jamie and Lorna, the receptionist from the Teen Center, laughing and talking. When Kathy, the front office manager, comes from the back office and relieves Jamie for her break, Jamie and Lorna walk away. Brooklin reminds Kathy, "The front desk clerks are the first personnel our visitors interact with and we have one opportunity to make a first impression. Please reinforce the lobby rules with your staff." Kathy is aware that Brooklin doesn't like staff members chatting at the front desk. Brooklin continues her walk and minutes later sees Jamie and Lorna walking into the courtyard.

When Brooklin returns to her office, Linda calls regarding the maids' dismissal. She informs Brooklin that everything went smoothly and Max had just escorted them out of the hotel. She also mentions that, "Joan was a little argumentative; however, I told her you had made this decision. I discussed the reason they were terminated and told them they were being paid through the end of the month. I have chosen two candidates to replace Mary and Joan whom I interviewed previously. I will have them come in tomorrow. Will you have time to talk to them tomorrow?" Linda asks.

Each supervisor interviews and recommends candidates for their department; however, Brooklin meets each applicant before they are offered the position to make certain they will complement the hotel's team. Brooklin tells Linda to have Erica block out some time for her to meet the candidates and thanks her for the call.

Brooklin gets ready to make another

call when she hears Linda talking to someone in her office. "I hear you. But, it's not difficult to work for Brooklin. She just wants the hotel to be a top quality hotel. I know it's a Five Star Hotel, but she wants to keep it that way. I really like her. Yes, I heard that too. Do you think there is a link between what happened to Larry and ..." There is silence and a disconnection. "No!" Brooklin says loudly to herself. "What happened and who was in the office with Linda? I only heard Linda's part of the conversation. And what was that about a link between what happened with Larry and what or who? Were they talking about a link between me and what happened to Larry? What is going on? Larry *did* say he needed to talk to me." Brooklin buzzes Erica and asks her to go immediately to Linda's office. She tells Erica she wants to know who is in Linda's office and to be anonymous. A couple minutes later, Brooklin hears a knock on her door and in walks Detective Ryan.

"Good afternoon, Ms. Covington. Do you have a few minutes to talk?" he asks. Brooklin thinks this man has a talent for appearing at the most undesirable times.

"Certainly," Brooklin says. "Come in! How is the questioning of our staff going?"

"Everything is going fine and I wanted to thank you and your staff for your hospitality. I told Kevin how much I enjoyed the food. I just passed Erica in the corridor and explained to her some of my interviews took longer than I expected; therefore, I will not be able to meet with all of the employees today. With your approval, I would like to return tomorrow to continue the meetings with your staff."

"That will be fine, Detective Ryan. However, I would like to make a request of you."

"And what is that?" he asks.

"I would like Logan Courtyard's name to remain out of the news. I do not want Logan Courtyard to be associated with what happened with Larry, especially now that the Teen Center's phonathon is this weekend. Is that possible?"

"For you, anything is possible. I will do my best to keep Logan Courtyard's name out of the media. Of course, that can change if we find evidence that someone at Logan Courtyard was driving the vehicle that hit

Larry."

"Thank you, Detective Ryan."

Detective Ryan reflects for a moment and says, "That is right, the Teen Center's Phonathon is this weekend. Good luck with it.

Again Brooklin says, "Thank you."

"Guess I'll see you again tomorrow." He stands, stretches and walks out of her office. Brooklin realizes she smells cologne. The scent is very unique, sensual, yet fresh and light. She doesn't remember Detective Ryan wearing cologne yesterday.

Erica returns interrupting Brooklin's thoughts. "Erica, who was in Linda's office?"

"No one, although I was delayed a few minutes by Detective Ryan informing me he needed to return tomorrow to complete his questioning. Oh, and I will tell Kevin to provide complimentary food again tomorrow for Detective Ryan. Now back to Linda," Erica says. "When I was half way to Linda's office, she was walking down the hall alone and I didn't see anyone in the hallway. I even lingered long enough for Linda to go into the ladies' room and sneaked a quick look in her office. After she returned to her office, I checked the ladies' room. No one was there. Why, what's going on?" she asks.

"That's what I'm trying to determine," Brooklin says.

Chapter 4

Hands full and still tired from the stress of yesterday, Brooklin struggles to unlock her office door. She turns and notices that her daughter Laila is right behind her. Laila laughs and asks, "Mom, need some help?"

Brooklin smiles, "Yes, Laila that would be nice." Laila takes her mother's keys, unlocks the door and removes one of the bags from her mother's hand. Brooklin gives Laila a hug and asks, "How's everything?"

"Everything is fine," Laila replies. "Just haven't seen you since last week. Want to go for a cup of coffee?"

"Absolutely," Brooklin says and they walk down to the restaurant. Laila is 5'6 and looks like Brooklin's twin except for the tattoos and her trendy style. Laila also definitely has her father's eyes and personality. They talk about how Laila's doing in school, her work at the Teen Center and Luke's injury. "So, how are you and Julie doing in the apartment without Luke?"

"Well, even before Luke injured his ankle, he was rarely at the apartment. I think he has a new girlfriend," Laila says.

"Really? Do you know who?"

"No. I guess he will tell me when he's ready," Laila adds.

"Do you think it's serious?"

"I don't know, Mom."

"Well, what about you? Have you started dating again since you and Brad decided to go your separate ways?"

"No, I'm not in any rush," she says.

"Well, that's smart." They talk for a few more minutes and walk to the hotel's favorite quiet place of escape, the terraced garden.

"Mom, this place is beautiful. Each time I visit the terrace, it seems more special. The stepping stones, the array of garden plants, flowers on arches, the wonderful blend of color and even the lavender scent throughout the garden. I love it!"

"Yes, the staff has done a wonderful job. The terrace is stunning yet it has a calming and soothing effect."

Laila and Brooklin continue talking and admiring the garden. After about fifteen minutes, they return to Brooklin's office. Taylor is standing at Erica's desk talking to her. Laila gives Brooklin a hug and says,

"Okay Mom, got to run now. Have to go to class."

"Laila, will you and Julie be at dinner on Sunday?" Brooklin asks.

"Yes, but I'll stop at the house tonight and check on Luke."

"Okay, I'll see you tonight and, Laila, thanks for the visit." Laila smiles, turns and walks through the double doors. As Brooklin walks toward her office, Taylor asks if she has a few minutes to meet with her. "Sure," Brooklin says.

Taylor updates Brooklin on hotel business and tells her that Carl changed Max from second to first shift security until Larry returns. Also Carl is using Howard who works per diem for second shift. "I talked to Detective Ryan earlier," says Taylor. "Erica tells me that he will finish questioning the staff tomorrow."

Brooklin tells Taylor, "I received a message from the Morning Herald newspaper this morning. They would like to hold a job fair here in August. I'll return their call today and pass along the information for you and Karen to work out the details. I would like to review the proposal before it is presented to the Morning Herald. Okay, Taylor, is there anything else?"

"No, I think that's it," she says.

"Oh, Taylor, how is the Guidelines and Attendance DVD coming?"

"I'm still working on it," she says.

"Okay, I would like to have the DVD completed by Monday for our meeting with Karen."

Brooklin buzzes Erica who tells her that the two housekeeping candidates have arrived. Brooklin tells her to give her about five minutes before sending in the first candidate. Brooklin watches as Taylor walks out and notices she is dressed unusually casual today. A silk, v-neck button down shirt, push-up bra and close-fitting capri pants with heels ... such a different look for Taylor. She looks younger.

Brooklin finishes interviewing and checks her messages. Colin called about ten minutes earlier. She returns Colin's call. "Hi, I'm sorry I missed your call. I was interviewing. Colin, we need to replace the little refrigerator in my office. I know Jerry from the restaurant is tired of bringing me bottled water."

"All right, Brooklin, we can get a new refrigerator for your office this weekend."

"Great," Brooklin says.

"Did Luke tell you his car was towed?" Colin asks.

"No," Brooklin responds. "When was his car towed?"

"Late Monday night. He asked me to go with him this morning to get his car. I went with him, paid the fee and left."

"You didn't wait for him?" Brooklin asks.

"No, I was told everything was fine. So, I left."

"Late Monday night? That's odd. That's the day he sprained his ankle. He was at home. Why would …" Brooklin pauses a moment. "Where was his car towed from?"

"I don't know, Brooklin."

"I thought his car was at his apartment. How has he been getting to school and work?" Brooklin asks.

"He told me he's been catching a ride with a friend."

"I think I will ask him to come down to my office and we can have a talk about what is going on with him. Colin, I didn't get a chance to talk to you last night about what happened here yesterday." Brooklin tells him about hearing Linda's conversation.

"You don't know who she was talking to?" he asks.

"No, I even sent Erica to Linda's office. When Erica arrived, no one was there," Brooklin says.

"Well, it seems as if Linda likes you, and the person she was talking to may not be as fond of you," he laughs.

"Colin, I don't think it's funny. I'm going to find the person who was in that office with Linda and learn what that conversation was about."

"I know you will," he says and she can hear the amusement in his voice. They talk for a few more minutes and she tells him about her conversation with Laila.

"Well, I know you enjoyed having a cup of coffee with your daughter."

"I did," Brooklin says. "You know, I love my kids. I also, love my husband. As a matter of fact, I'm coming home a little early tonight. What about you?" Brooklin asks.

"What time is early, Brooklin?"

She answers, "5:30."

Colin says, "I'll see you then." Smiling, Brooklin places the phone on the desk. Then she thinks about Luke and calls his cell phone. No answer. Brooklin buzzes Erica and tell her that she's trying to locate Luke.

"Okay," Erica replies, "I'll track him down."

"Thanks. Oh and Erica, can you please bring me a bottled water?"

About fifteen minutes later, Luke walks in Brooklin's office. She notices he is walking almost normal with the ankle brace. "Hi, Mom, you were looking for me?"

"Hi, Luke, and yes, I was looking for you. Your father told me your car was towed Monday night."

"Yes," he says slowly, his face flushed.

"Luke, what happened?"

"I didn't see the 'No Parking' sign," he says "and my car was towed."

"Luke, I'm confused. Monday night, you were at home. That was the day you sprained your ankle. I brought you home from the hospital."

"I know, Mom. I remembered something I had to take care of, and I left home for a couple of hours."

"You left home? You felt well enough to leave home?"

"Yes, I wore my ankle brace."

"Where did you go? What was so important? "

"Does it really matter, Mom?"

"Luke, I think I asked where did you go? And if your car was towed, how did you get home?"

"Mom, why are you all in my business? I'm 21 years old. I have to go." Luke walks toward the door.

"Luke," Brooklin calls but he walks out of her office. Brooklin's mouth drops open. She is stunned. Brooklin's thinks to herself, "What just happened? And, I didn't have the opportunity to ask if he has a new girlfriend. Well, Mr. 21 year old Luke, your father and I are going to have a long conversation with you. And we will want answers." Erica walks in with Brooklin's bottled water. Brooklin laughs and says, "Did I ask for bottled water or a glass of wine? I think I need a glass of wine right now."

"Do you want me to get you a glass of wine?"

"No, I'm just joking. You know I don't drink at work," Brooklin says.

"Well, there is always a first time," Erica says. "And hey, I was going to have a glass with you," and they both laugh.

Brooklin's door is open and Detective Ryan walks in, "It sounds like you two are enjoying your day."

"Hi, Detective Ryan," Erica says as she walks to the door and closes it behind her.

"Hi, Erica," and he turns to Brooklin. "Hello, Ms. Covington."

"Detective Ryan," Brooklin says.

"Well, I have interviewed your full staff."

"Can I ask about your conclusions?"

"What would you like to know, Ms. Covington?" he says with a smile.

"Do you think Larry was hit intentionally? Do you think someone here is responsible?" she asks curiously.

"Normally, I wouldn't say this to a woman who is as beautiful and gorgeous as you, but slow down," he says with a mischievous grin.

"Detective Ryan," Brooklin begins and he holds up his hand to stop her from continuing.

"Wait, I'm just giving you a compliment. A well-deserved one, I must say. However, back to this case, I have just begun my investigation. I don't know the answer to your questions yet. I do have other individuals outside of Logan Courtyard that I have to question. But I promise to keep you informed. Besides, it will give me an excuse to come back to see you." He laughs and adds, "I'm just joking."

"I hope so, Detective, because I am married."

"Yes, I know. Mr. Covington is a very lucky man." He stands and moves to the door. "I'll talk to you soon, Ms. Covington" and closes the door behind him.

Detective Ryan leaves Logan Courtyard en route to Waters Avenue on the south side. He parks his unmarked vehicle and leisurely walks to the corner store. He makes eye contact with Corey who is standing in front of the store, enters and proceeds to the coolers in the rear of the small market. He returns to the front of the store and purchases a Pepsi. He leaves the mini mart, walks to his vehicle and a few minutes later, Corey slides in the back seat.

"What's up, Detective? I have places to be."

"What's the word on the street about Larry Carter?"

"You haven't closed that case yet?"

"Don't act ignorant, Corey. Answer the question."

"My boys told me Larry owed Big Mel money and if you don't pay up, you might get some broken bones or be found floating face down. Does that answer your question?"

"Corey, where can I find Big Mel these days?"

"Lately, he's been hanging out at Grill 55 on Geer Blvd. Now, can you stop this car and let me out? My boys have low tolerance for guys who talk to the cops."

Erica stands in the doorway of Brooklin's office, "There is a Mr. Dalton in the lobby who would like to talk to you. He said he was referred by the mayor."

Brooklin is surprised, "The mayor?" She thinks for a few seconds. "Well, I was en route to the restaurant to get a cup of tea.

However, I can stop in the lobby first."

As Brooklin closes her office door, Erica emerges with a small framed man who looks to be in his mid-fifties dressed in a dark blue suit. She asks him to have a seat. She walks over and whispers to Brooklin, "Jamie sent him to my office."

"Okay, I will have to speak to Kathy regarding her staff sending guests to areas of the hotel before consent is given," Brooklin says in a low tone.

Erica walks over to the gentleman and introduces him to Brooklin. "Ms. Covington, this is Mr. Dalton." He stands and extends his hand. Erica observes them as they exchange greetings.

"Mr. Dalton, would you like to accompany me to our restaurant for a cup of coffee or tea?"

"Ms. Covington, yes, I would like a cup of coffee." Mr. Dalton and Brooklin sit in the section of the restaurant that normally doesn't open until lunchtime. "Ms. Covington, I am an FBI agent," he says as he reaches in his suit pocket and displays his badge. "The mayor was gracious enough to allow me to use his name because I didn't have an appointment. I am here to ask if the FBI can house a young man who is in our Witness Protection program here at Logan Courtyard for approximately two weeks." Brooklin is a little stunned by this request. "Logan Courtyard was chosen because of its location, floor plan and, of course, its reputation. We would like to use the entire 11th floor if possible."

"You would like to use the entire 11th floor?"

"Yes. And, of course, Logan Courtyard will be well compensated."

"Agent Dalton, I would think the FBI would choose a private remote location to house a witness."

"That's exactly what we would like people to think. However, each circumstance is different. Ms. Covington, if you are concerned about a disturbance occurring at Logan Courtyard, let me put your mind at ease. You and your staff will not even know we are here."

"When would you like this guest to arrive?"

"Tomorrow."

"Tomorrow? We cannot possibly

accommodate you. We have guests who have made advance reservations and I will not cancel those reservations."

"Ms. Covington, what arrangements can be made for this gentleman? We would like him to be housed here at Logan Courtyard."

"There is one suite on each floor that is set apart from the other suites," she explains. On the eleventh floor, it is Suite 1107. We can offer this suite to you. It's a two bedroom suite located at the end of the hallway, and it's actually situated around the corner from the other suites on the floor. Therefore, it will provide some privacy. "

"May I take a look at the suite?"

"Certainly. If you will give me a few minutes, I will obtain the key card from the front office." As Brooklin walks through the hallway, she telephones her attorney, Levy, on her work cell. She briefs him on this development and asks him to verify that a Mr. Dalton is with the FBI. She also asks Levy to email to her cell a photo of Mr. Dalton as soon as possible. After her conversation with Levy, she enters the front office and obtains the key card from the cabinet.

She and Agent Dalton take the elevator to the eleventh floor. They walk through the suite. He shows no emotion as he examines each room and the impressive views of the beach from the suite's many windows. Brooklin's phone vibrates and she reads the email from Levy. Mr. Dalton *is* with the FBI. She scrolls down and sees the photo of the man who is standing before her. They return to the sitting room and Agent Dalton says, "Ms. Covington, we will accept this suite. It will work well for us. If at all possible, we would like our witness, Mr. Reed, to arrive tomorrow morning around 5am with two agents who will be dressed in plain clothes."

"That will be fine. I brought the necessary pre-registration paperwork with me. Would you like to take a few minutes to complete the registration information now?"

"Yes, certainly."

"Good, then tomorrow morning the agents and Mr. Reed can go directly to Suite 1107 upon their arrival."

"That is perfect, Ms. Covington. Now, we must ask you to not divulge this information to anyone including family members or anyone on your staff. We do not want our witness to be placed in any danger or his whereabouts known. He is needed to testify in a highly classified court case."

"Agent Dalton, if Mr. Reed is to reside in the hotel, I must confide in our attorney."

Agent Dalton interrupts Brooklin and says, "We expected you would confide in Atty. Levy Jones and this is agreeable to us. However, we would ask that you entrust this information only with Atty. Jones and, of course, we informed the mayor." Brooklin completes the registration for the suite and provides Agent Dalton with the key cards. They agree on a scenario to provide to hotel personnel regarding the three guests in Room 1107. Brooklin explains to Agent Dalton that the hotel staff signs a non-disclosure agreement. Therefore, the FBI will have the privacy and discretion they require.

"Yes, Ms. Covington, we are aware of Logan Courtyard's confidentiality statement. I would like to thank you again for your hospitality and for the suite."

"You are welcome, Agent Dalton." He nods and walks to the elevator. Brooklin takes a different elevator to her office. Today she would like to enjoy a few minutes with her private thoughts.

When Brooklin returns to her office, she is relieved that Erica is not at her desk. A few minutes later, Erica walks in her office, closes the door and asks, "Is everything okay?"

"Yes, Erica. Why would you think otherwise?"

"That Mr. Dalton seemed a little weird."

"Erica, please. He was not weird. Our mayor was kind enough to refer three business associates to Logan Courtyard. They will spend the next couple of weeks working on a project for the mayor. We didn't have any available rooms; therefore, they will be in Suite 1107. Oh Erica, I forgot to mention that I'm going to the Teen Center tomorrow morning and I'll return to Logan Courtyard after lunch." Brooklin pauses and then says, "And Erica, I need you to make certain everything is set for our phonathon guests tomorrow."

"I'll be sure to take care of it," Erica says as she walks toward the door.

Chapter 5

Brooklin stops at Memorial Hospital Friday morning to check on Larry before going to the Teen Center. She has not heard from Mark, although staff members are saying there hasn't been any change in Larry's condition. She walks directly to the Trauma Center ICU and finds the waiting room is empty. She waits about five minutes and then presses the buzzer to the Trauma Center ICU. A female voice asks, "May I help you?"

"I would like to visit Larry Carter."

"Are you a member of his family?"

"No, I'm his employer."

"I'm sorry, only family is permitted visitation with Mr. Carter."

"Is Mr. Carter's brother, Mark, visiting?"

"No, Mr. Carter does not have any visitors at this time."

"Can you tell me how Mr. Carter is progressing?"

"Sorry, we cannot provide any information."

Brooklin leaves ICU and telephones Erica. She asks Erica to call Mark, tell him she was at the hospital today to visit Larry, and ask him to give her a call. She briefly checks for important messages then heads for the Teen Center.

Colin and Brooklin take great pride in the Center that provides 13-18 year old teens an afterschool program during the week and on weekends is open from 11am – 11pm. Programs include tutoring, mentoring, field trips, specialty classes, various competitions and college scholarships. The site contains a library, computer room, game room, cafeteria, weight room and gym with a basketball court. Also there is an outdoor swimming pool, football field, and party room. The Center is supported through fund-raisers and a yearly phonathon. This year, Colin and Brooklin hope to add an indoor pool, an outdoor track to the football field and some needed repairs to the Center. Laila works part-time at the Center. Brooklin volunteers a half-day during the week and a half-day on Saturdays. Parents, individuals from various organizations, community members, and churches are part of the volunteer staff sharing their expertise with the kids. Volunteers, staff at the Teen Center and Logan Courtyard employees are required to complete a background investigation before volunteering or beginning their employment. Lorna currently schedules the Teen Center's volunteers.

As Brooklin is leaving her car at the Teen Center, she reaches for her cell phone and notices she has a message. "Hi, Mom, it's Luke. I'm calling to apologize for yesterday. I'm sorry, I have a lot going on right now. But, that's no excuse. I love you and I'll talk to you soon." An apology from Luke? Wow, that was pretty nice, she thinks. Lately, her days seem to be filled with a lot of anxiety. That message was a welcome change.

As Brooklin enters the Teen Center, a smile materializes. It looks absolutely wonderful. The facility is always clean and neat, but today it looks as if a professional prepared it for the phonathon. Brooklin glances at Lorna who is sitting behind the desk. "Wow," she says to Lorna. "It looks amazing!"

Lorna replies, "I know. Colin spoke to Maple Furniture yesterday and they sent four of their staff members with a truckload of furniture. You're looking at the end results."

"Well, I love it. Did they donate the furniture?"

"Yes," Lorna says, "they donated all the furniture. You have to take a tour. They placed furniture throughout the building, changing the look of each room."

"Well, they did an outstanding job. Is Colin here?"

"Yes, he's in his office."

Brooklin walks down the hall to Colin's office looking in each room along the way. She spots Colin and gives him a quick kiss on the cheek. "Why didn't you tell me Maple Furniture donated furnishings and changed the look of this place?"

"I wanted to surprise you," Colin says.

"Well, the place looks great." Brooklin sits down and asks, "Are we ready for tomorrow?"

"As ready as we are going to be." Colin has invited the mayor and his wife, community leaders, company executives, individuals from numerous organizations, staff from area schools, friends and several Teen Center's parents to work the phonathon. He also invited two pro football players from the Baltimore area, who will be Logan

Courtyard's guests while working the phonathon. As they leave Colin's office, Brooklin tells him about the voice mail from Luke. "Good, I had planned to talk to him about his behavior," he says as they enter the conference room to discuss tomorrow's phonathon.

It's early afternoon when Brooklin returns to Logan Courtyard. In her voice mail she finds a message from Agent Dalton informing her all is well. She thinks about this situation and hopes she won't regret allowing the FBI access to Logan Courtyard. A few minutes later, Erica informs her Mark phoned when she was at the Teen Center. He said he's sorry he missed her at the hospital but Larry's condition hasn't changed. He remains in a coma. Brooklin unlocks her office door, walks in and slumps down in the chair. After a few minutes, she turns to the window and looks down at the courtyard with its beauty and pure, unadulterated serenity.

Brooklin is lost in thought when she hears someone calling her name. "Brooklin!" She turns and sees Meghan from accounting. "Hi, I knocked, but you didn't hear me. Sorry to interrupt, but Erica isn't at her desk and your door was open." Meghan hesitates a moment and then says, "We have a payroll meeting scheduled. Is this still a good time for you to meet?"

"Yes, Meghan, come in." She places the payroll folder in front of Brooklin. Meghan handles all accounting functions for the hotel and Teen Center. Lorna provides Meghan with the Teen Center's payroll information and Meghan computes all payrolls. Colin and Brooklin have given strict instructions that the Teen Center and Logan Courtyard accounts must be kept separate. However, Brooklin oversees all accounting matters and sign all checks for the hotel and Teen Center.

Brooklin works about an hour after her meeting with Meghan. Erica informs her that the limo has arrived with the two NFL players. Brooklin had given specific instructions for their VIP treatment. She walks into the lobby where Colin is talking to the two men. He places his arm around her waist and introduces her. Brooklin welcomes them to Logan Courtyard, and the four of them walk to Meeting Room One where the press awaits them. They face the media for thirty minutes answering a barrage of questions. With the press conference completed, the players are escorted to their plush VIP suites. The players have about two hours before the limo will transport them to the Teen Center to talk to the kids followed by a Meet-and-Greet session for those fortunate enough to have tickets. By the end of the night, Brooklin's face hurts from smiling. However, all went well. The kids were wonderful and asked great questions, and the football players demonstrated some great football techniques for the kids. They were gracious in giving autographs and posing for photos. The publicity and exposure on the evening news will help tomorrow's phonathon fundraiser. Brooklin returns to Colin's office, gathers her things and walks out of the Teen Center. She is absolutely exhausted.

The next morning, Colin, Luke, Laila, Julie and Brooklin arrive at the Teen Center at 5am ready to begin their work on the phonathon. Erica rushes over to tell Brooklin about the night back at Logan Courtyard. The NFL players were in the VIP section of the bar where they apparently invited a few people to party with them until around 3am.

After hearing about their night, Brooklin is hoping they will arrive before the phonathon begins at 7am.

At 6:45am, the two players walk into the Center. Colin briefs them, and all the volunteers take their seats, collect their scripts, pick up the telephone and begin calling at 7am. They take breaks, eat, converse with each other and begin calling again.

During Brooklin's last break, she notices Lorna sitting at a table in the back of the cafeteria having a sandwich and a diet soda. She decides to have a conversation with her. "So, Lorna, you spent your day off at the hotel Wednesday," Brooklin says smiling and sitting in the chair across from Lorna.

Lorna laughs, "Yes, almost the entire day."

"Yes, I saw you talking to Jamie earlier in the day and later around 2:30, I noticed you were in Linda's office."

Lorna looks a little surprised and then says, "Yes, I *was* in Linda's office, but I'm not sure what time it was."

"Oh, I'm certain it was around 2:30 because I happened to look at my watch when

I saw Mary and Joan leaving Linda's office," Brooklin adds.

"Oh, yes, that's right," Lorna says. "I met them when they were coming out of Linda's office with Max," she says carefully, looking a little confused. "You were near Linda's office? I thought she telephoned you," Lorna says. Then she stops abruptly, looking a little awkward.

Brooklin thinks, "Wow, thanks Lorna for volunteering that bit of information." Brooklin continues, "Oh she *did* telephone me," Brooklin says smiling, "however when I'm out of my office, I transfer my calls to my work cell phone." Brooklin knows Lorna would not have any way of knowing that she wasn't being truthful. Lorna presents a ghost of a smile and nods. So, it was Lorna in Linda's office talking about her. That was easy. Now she has to let Detective Ryan know he needs to have a little talk with Lorna. Thereafter, Brooklin will deal with Ms. Lorna.

After returning to her seat and preparing to make her next call, Brooklin is still distracted about her conversation with Lorna. She takes a minute to collect herself and re-focuses on the Teen Center. Brooklin tells herself that she will have time after the phonathon to handle this matter. At that moment, another news reporter arrives to tape a segment for the evening news. At 7pm, the phonathon ends; they have surpassed their goal of $200,000 and reached a total of $220,000. The celebration begins. Champagne from Logan Courtyard arrives, and the volunteers eat, drink and rejoice. Colin and Brooklin thank everyone for their time, donations and assistance. The mayor expresses his gratitude and reports that the dropout rate in the local high school is lower largely due to the Center. The mayor ends with a toast to the Teen Center and its staff. They return to Logan Courtyard's banquet room with the football players who promise to volunteer at the Teen Center two days during their off season. Colin and Brooklin thank everyone again and excuse themselves just before midnight. They arrive at home, shower, and collapse in bed.

The next morning Brooklin awakes to the sound of the television downstairs. She rushes through her morning routine, grabs her housecoat and joins Colin and Laila. They relax as they watch the weekend morning programs and discuss last night events. Colin decides to have dinner delivered today and says, "I'm sure everyone is probably still tired from the phonathon. We can just have a lazy day."

"So, what are we going to order for dinner?" Laila asks.

"Why don't you and Julie decide," responds Colin.

"So, the decision is to order dinner?" Julie asks as she returns to the family room.

"Yes," Laila says, "What would you like to eat?" They continue to discuss food, school and work.

Brooklin asks Laila if Luke is coming for dinner today.

"I don't know," she says. "Luke wasn't home when I left."

"Laila, did Luke come home last night?" Colin asks. She shakes her head "no" and mentions how Luke told her at the phonathon last night that he wasn't coming home.

Colin looks at Laila and then at Brooklin. He grabs his cell phone and calls Luke. Luke answers, says he won't be home for dinner today. He mentions that he forgot about plans he made previously to hang out with the guys. Colin chides Luke for not letting them know he wouldn't be home for dinner.

Later Brooklin is in bed and eagerly waiting for Colin to join her. She sits up when he walks to the bed. He looks at her inquisitively as she tells him about her conversation with Lorna at the phonathon. "Really?" he says. "You really think Lorna is the person who was discussing you in Linda's office?"

"Colin, she practically admitted it," Brooklin says.

"What are you going to do now?" he asks.

"I'm going to have a talk with Detective Ryan and ask him to question Lorna. He needs to question her regarding any information she may have concerning Larry's case."

"Brooklin, let the detective work the case. I want you to stay out of it," he insists.

"I'm just providing him with some details. Remember, Larry is one of our employees."

"So is Lorna and a very good worker, I

might add," he says.

"Maybe not for long," Brooklin says.

Colin looks at her and just shakes his head.

Chapter 6

At Monday's weekly staff meeting, everyone is offering their congratulations on the phonathon's successful outcome. Brooklin thanks them and moves quickly into staff conversations. Tom informs everyone that Lee, the second shift maintenance worker, had fallen down a flight of stairs at his home and broke his leg, making maintenance down one man. He explains that Harvey was changed to second shift and the temp employment agency is sending three candidates for third shift maintenance tomorrow. Brooklin suggests that one of the groundsmen works overnight maintenance until Lee returns and that a part-time temp be hired for the grounds work. She tells Meghan that they will discuss payroll issues later.

Brooklin has another meeting scheduled in thirty minutes and returns to her office thinking she will grab a bottle of water from her new office refrigerator and freshen up as well. She finds Andy from maintenance emptying her garbage can. "Hi, Ms. Brooklin, normally your office is cleaned overnight, but we are down one man in maintenance."

"Hi, Andy, Tom informed me about Lee during our meeting. Please continue. I'll only be here a few minutes. I have another meeting to attend."

Andy studies Brooklin carefully and says, "How are you doing Ms. Brooklin? I hope you aren't stressed about all that's going on here at Logan."

"What are you referring to, Andy?"

"You know - with all that's happening with Larry," he turns around to look at Brooklin.

"Andy, do you know any details about what happened to Larry?"

"Ms. Brooklin, I work maintenance. We see and hear a lot. But, you know, I'm close to my retirement and I just keep my mouth shut."

"Andy," Brooklin says, "you can trust me. What have you heard?"

At that moment Brooklin sees Jamie at the door who says, "Erica asked me to tell you that your guests arrived early and will be in Conference Room Two."

"Okay," Brooklin says. She turns back to Andy and says, "Before you leave today, I would like to finish our conversation." He gives a serious nod and goes on with his rounds. Brooklin takes a few minutes to freshen up her makeup and then walks to the conference room thinking about her talk with Andy. Maybe finally, she will get some answers.

In the conference room Brooklin sees two well dressed women conversing with Erica. She introduces herself, extends her hand to each and sits down. The ladies, Veronica and Marion, both look to be in their mid-forties. Brooklin listens and observes attentively as they present their proposal. Logan Courtyard has space for an additional tenant, and Erica had provided the ladies with a quick tour of the hotel and the available space before Brooklin arrived at the meeting. Veronica and Marion express their desire to have a unique gift shop in Logan Courtyard that would include a line of edible merchandise called 'YumMe'. Veronica displays some of the edible merchandise that would be available. Marion shows a portfolio with pages of beautiful gift ideas, products that are "tasteful" and some that are "tasty" – all elegantly packaged. Brooklin informs the women that a few other businesses are interested in the space and she thanks them for coming. Before they exit, Veronica turns to Brooklin and says, "This is one of the finest hotels in this area and in the state. One hotel review states that guests are elevated by the experience of even one night at Logan Courtyard. Ms. Covington, just think how your guests' will delight in our products here at Logan Courtyard." Brooklin thanks them again.

Erica walks them to the lobby, returns to Brooklin's office, and says with a big grin, "What do you think?"

"I think you should not discuss this with anyone because I have not made a decision."

"But are you leaning" and she leans forward, "in the direction of a yes?" she asks smiling.

Brooklin laughs and says, "I'm unsure, but I think I can tell what *you* think we should do."

She says, "Yes, no other hotel I know has edible merchandise and I'm sure a lot of our guests would welcome the stimulation," she laughs.

"Well, Colin and I will discuss it along with the other businesses interested in the space. Now, I need to make a personal phone call. Can you give me about fifteen minutes and then call my brother Jim and ask him to come down to my office?"

Brooklin telephones her friend Jill who owns a permanent employment agency. "Hi, Jill, it's Brooklin, how are you?" They talk for a few minutes, discussing an opening for an office worker with light accounting skills. Brooklin provides her with information regarding the position. They agree that the candidates will arrive at the hotel tomorrow at 7pm. Brooklin explains that her secretary leaves at 5pm; therefore, the candidates should ask for her at the front desk. There is a knock on her door. "Okay, Jill, I will talk to you soon."

Brooklin tells Erica to hold her calls while she meets with Jim. It's Monday morning and Jim looks like he has slept in an abandoned tenement house. Of course, she knows he hasn't, given that Jim lives in Colin's old duplex. They only charge him $200 a month for rent in an attempt to make him responsible. They actually had to begin deducting the rent money from his pay check; otherwise, they wouldn't receive the payments. Brooklin's thoughts return to her recent telephone conversation with the tenant who lives upstairs from Jim. He informed her that Jim was home with some woman for about four or five days. You mean Kelly?" Brooklin asked.

"No," replied the tenant, "he was with some other woman. They both were drunk."

"Jim," Brooklin asks, "can you please tell me why you haven't been at work?"

"I've been having some problems – some personal problems."

"Jim," Brooklin says, "I can't help if you don't tell me what is going on."

"Who said I needed your help?" he says hoarsely.

"Jim, watch your tone of voice. I'm trying to retain you as an employee but you're making it very difficult."

"Retain me as an employee? You can't fire me. This hotel is as much mine as it is yours. This is my mother's hotel and I don't know why Mom …" Frustrated, he pauses and says, "Just forget it."

"Okay, starting today, you will be paid

only for the hours you work. You will no longer be a salaried employee. If you do not clear enough money to pay your rent, you will be evicted. I am also placing you on probation for 60 days. If you miss any days during this probationary period, you will be terminated. Furthermore, you are being temporarily transferred to the grounds department. Lee in maintenance broke his leg, and we have transferred a grounds worker to maintenance until Lee returns. So, starting tomorrow, report to Tom for your assignment. I don't want to hear about any problems regarding your work performance. If problems arise, you'll be immediately terminated. Are we clear on this, Jim?"

"I can't believe you are doing this to me. This is embarrassing," he says.

Brooklin continues, "You should be embarrassed about your habits, work ethics, Jim, and of course your appearance. Now, sign this probationary letter." He doesn't move. "If you don't sign the letter, you will be terminated."

"Why do I have to work for the grounds department?"

"It's either the grounds department or

the Teen Center. And you know, Colin will not tolerate any inappropriate behavior or you not showing for work."

"I think I'd rather work for the Teen Center," says Jim. "What type of work would I be doing at the Teen Center?"

Brooklin replies, "That's for Colin to decide. However, you still have to sign the probationary letter." He grabs the letter, signs it and slinks toward the door. "Jim, you need to report to work tomorrow at the Teen Center at 10am."

"Fine," he says. As he exits, Brooklin thinks about Colin. Oh, he is going to love her for sending him Jim. She'll tell him tonight and she smiles.

Brooklin walks to the restaurant and orders lunch. She feels the need to leave her office and breathe in some fresh air. She takes her lunch, today's newspaper and sits at a small table in the courtyard. She looks at the beach's crystal clear water and after a few minutes, begins to relax.

After lunch as Brooklin takes her daily walk around the hotel, she decides to stop in each area and talk to the employees. She thinks about her earlier conversation with

Andy and realizes each employee has something to add to the mix. She spends the majority of her day having discussions with the supervisors and her personal staff. Today, she is embarking on a new approach.

As she enters the maintenance department, she stops and looks for Andy. He, of course, isn't in the area. She calls his extension on her cell. He answers and says he is returning to the maintenance area now. As she looks into the staff parking lot, she remembers a couple of months earlier stopping here and noticing a blue car in the parking lot, she thinks a Mazda 626. Could that have been the car that hit Larry? She remembers the car because it was an odd color blue. It looked like the owner had painted the car rather than a professional factory paint job. She sees Andy approaching and asks him if he knows who drives a blue Mazda. Maybe, a Mazda 626?

He shakes his head and says, "No, I don't, Ms. Brooklin. Is there a problem?"

"No," Brooklin says. "Andy, I would like to finish our earlier conversation. Have you heard anything about what happened to Larry or seen anything?"

"I don't want to get in the middle of any disputes, Ms. Brooklin."

"I understand that, Andy. However, you can confide in me."

Andy smiles warmly and says, "I do trust you, Ms. Brooklin. What I heard was that the hit and run was intentional. People don't pay much attention to the maintenance staff. It's like we are invisible. I normally don't repeat what I hear because I don't want any trouble," he says.

"Have you heard anyone say who was driving the car?"

"No, they were saying it could be a number of people. Larry apparently was sleeping with a lot of women and they said some were married."

"Did you tell Detective Ryan this when you talked to him?"

"No, I told him I didn't know anything."

"Andy, can you tell me who you overheard talking?"

"Ms. Brooklin, I really don't want to say anymore."

"I understand, Andy. Thanks for telling me what you heard. I will share this information with Detective Ryan. However, I won't tell him who told me."

"Thanks, Ms. Brooklin. I appreciate your not mentioning my name to the detective." Andy is being cautious and Brooklin doesn't want to press him for more details. She would like staff to feel comfortable sharing information with her regarding Logan Courtyard. Brooklin smiles thinking, "Andy and I made some progress today. It's a good beginning."

Chapter 7

Brooklin buzzes Erica and tells her to prepare a letter to Veronica and Marion thanking them for their interest in leasing space at the hotel but advising them that Logan Courtyard is declining their proposal. Last night, Colin and Brooklin discussed Veronica and Marion's proposal. Colin wondered why Brooklin appropriated time for this meeting, since normally Taylor would be responsible for such a meeting. However, Brooklin explained she needed Taylor's involvement in another project. Brooklin tells Colin that although the venture is not for Logan Courtyard she thinks the proposal is a good concept. Then they discuss Brooklin's thoughts on how Logan Courtyard should utilize the space.

Earlier this morning, Tom informed Brooklin that Larry's son Ron is looking for work and is interested in the temporary grounds worker's position. Tom noted the kid doesn't have experience in the job market but feels he would be a good worker. Brooklin signals Erica to send Ron in. "Hi" he says in a low tone. He is a nice looking young man dressed in a button down shirt and khaki pants.

"Hi, Ron, how are you?"

"Good," he says, looking down.

"Ron, we all were very sorry to hear about what happened to your father. How is he doing?"

"Not good. He's still in a coma."

"Well, we are praying he will get better soon. Now Ron, tell me a little about you."

He looks down at his hands and says, "I'm nineteen years old. I finished high school in May."

"You graduated from high school. Congratulations, that is a major accomplishment. What was your favorite subject in school?"

He looks at Brooklin momentarily, "Math was my favorite subject."

"Math? Actually, math was *my* favorite subject in school as well." Ron looks at Brooklin smiling. "What kind of grades did you receive in school?"

"I had a 3.2 average."

"Wow, Ron, that's fantastic. Were you involved in any clubs or afterschool activities?"

"No, I wasn't."

"You weren't? Why not?"

"I don't know."

"Did you have many friends in school?"

"No, I wasn't popular. The kids at school teased me."

"They teased you? What did they say?"

He looks down and says, "They would call me names."

"In middle school?"

"Mostly. But I was teased some in high school too. I was always like an outsider."

"Ron, those kids who teased you were exhibiting cowardly behavior. I'm sorry you had to experience that harassment. They missed an opportunity to have a good friend. I think you are a smart and handsome young man."

Ron smiles and says, "Thank you."

"You are welcome and I hope you know that people single out, talk about or hassle those they are intimidated by or because of jealousy. However, Ron, in spite of the stressful environment at school, you graduated with a 3.2 average. That demonstrates your strength and ability to overcome obstacles. Now that you have completed high school and creating a new path, tell me why you'd like to work for Logan Courtyard?"

"My father always loved working at Logan Courtyard. He always talked about how great it was to work at the hotel and how nice the people are."

"That's good to hear, Ron. What are your plans for the future?"

"I would like to take some business courses at the community college. But I need to earn some money first."

"Well, let's see what we can do to help you with that goal. It was very nice to meet you and Tom will be contacting you in a few days."

"Thanks, Ms. Brooklin." She notices a little pep in Ron's walks as he leaves the office. Hopefully, he'll develop into a confident young man. Brooklin calls Tom and tells him to move forward in bringing Ron on board if all goes well with the background clearance. Then she calls Taylor and gives her the information regarding hiring Ron and asks her to contact Tom to make certain it's a smooth transition.

Brooklin informs Erica that she has to return home for a short time and asks her to check the computerized records for the employee who drives a blue Mazda. "Is there a problem?" Erica asks.

"No," Brooklin says, "I just need that information."

"Okay, Brooklin, I'm on it." Brooklin had only left the office about twenty minutes when Detective Ryan walks through the doors asking for her. "I'm sorry Detective Ryan, Ms. Covington will be out of the hotel for a couple of hours. Would you like Ms. Covington to call you when she returns?"

"No, Erica, I will talk to Ms. Covington later." As he leaves Erica's office, his cell rings. A woman voice says, "Detective Ryan, I saw the news report on Mr. Carter's hit and run. I may have some information about the case."

"I'm sorry I didn't get your name."

"My name is Debra Williams."

"Ms. Williams, what information do you have regarding Mr. Carter's case?"

"I was pumping gas at a station on Bauknight Ferry on that Monday night, March

24th. I looked toward the street when I heard tires squealing and an engine roaring. I saw a car swerve and skid sideways off the road."

"Did you see who was driving the car?"

"I couldn't see who was driving. However, I think there were two people in the car."

"Did you see the vehicle hit Mr. Carter?"

"No, I didn't. That's the reason I didn't report it. I didn't see Mr. Carter. I just thought the driver lost control of the car. I left the following day for a business trip. I returned yesterday, heard about what happened to Mr. Carter and I called you."

"What type of car did you see swerve off the road?"

"It was a mid-size blue car. I'm not sure the type of car."

"Why do you think this was the car that hit Mr. Carter?"

"The news reporter on television said she was presently reporting from the crime scene. And the gas station is almost directly across from where she was standing."

"What happened after the car skidded off the road?"

"After about a minute the car pulled back on the road and continued down Bauknight Ferry."

"Do you remember anything else?"

"No, that's all I saw."

"And you think there were two people in the car?"

"It was dark, but I'm sure I saw two people in the car."

Detective Ryan thanks Ms. Williams for calling, verifies her telephone number and asks her to call him if she remembers more details. He checks his watch and remembers he has a meeting at the precinct. He realizes he will not be able to return to Logan Courtyard in the next couple of hours when Ms. Covington returns or even in the next few days. He wants to inquire if she had any new leads regarding Larry's case.

Luke walks into the kitchen as Colin is about to enter the garage to place his golf clubs in the car. "Hi, Dad."

"Hi, Luke, I'm going to the driving range to hit a bucket of balls. Would you like to join me?"

"Sure, Dad, I think my ankle has healed

enough so that I can practice my swing." Colin tries to play golf as much as possible without it interfering with his work at the Teen Center. And a morning on the driving range with his son will be great. Plus, it will give him the opportunity to learn what is happening with Luke.

Luke and Colin walk down to the tees, and Colin takes a few practice swings. Luke places a ball on the tee, swings his club but misses the ball. Colin tells Luke to concentrate on the ball at all times. "It's not how hard you swing; it's about keeping your eye on the ball," Colin says. Luke does and hits the golf ball about 100 yards. "Luke, don't swing your body to the left or the right when you swing the club. Swing the golf club smoothly and straight at the golf ball, rotating your hips." Colin demonstrates as he hits the ball about 250 yards. Luke takes his father's advice and hits the ball about 150 yards. "Great job, son." Luke smiles, relaxes and begin to hit one ball after the other. They finish one bucket of balls and purchase a second. "Luke," Colin says, "we haven't seen you very much lately. Are you dating anyone?"

Luke looks at Colin and asks, "Did Laila tell you I was seeing someone?"

"Laila doesn't have to tell me you are seeing someone. I'm a man and I know when a man is nowhere to be found as often as you have been, son, then, it's because of a woman."

"Yes, Dad, I'm seeing someone. I'm not sure where this relationship is headed, so I'm not ready to introduce her to you and Mom yet."

"Okay, Luke, I trust you're not getting into something that you will regret later. And I know you realize how important it is to always practice safe sex," Colin says.

"Dad, please."

"All right, I'm done. Let's finish this bucket of balls and go in the club house and grab a quick lunch."

Brooklin returns home to retrieve some paperwork and decides to have lunch while she's home. She kicks off her shoes and walks into the kitchen. Brooklin makes herself a large salad with almost every veggie she can find in the refrigerator. She grabs a bottle of water and goes into the family room to watch television. Colin and Luke walk in as she's sitting on the couch with her lunch. "Hi, Mom," Luke says.

"Hi," Brooklin says. "This is a surprise." Luke smiles and tells her that he and Colin spent a couple of hours at the driving range.

Colin smiles and asks, "Hi, honey, what are you doing home?"

"I came home for some paperwork I forgot this morning and decided to have a salad at home."

"Well, I'm going to run upstairs and get a shower. Are you going to be here in about twenty minutes?"

"No, I'm getting ready to return to the hotel now. I have two people to interview." Colin looks at Brooklin puzzled and she tells him, they can talk about it tonight.

"Mom, Dad, I gotta run," Luke says and hurries out the door.

After he leaves, Brooklin realizes and says to Colin, "I didn't see Luke's car outside. How is he traveling?"

"Good question, I don't know," says Colin as he looks out the window.

"Well, he's gone now. Perhaps he's

using Laila's car?"

"After I get dressed, I'll call Laila. But for now, I have to get in the shower. I'm going to be late for a meeting at the Teen Center," says Colin.

Brooklin kisses Colin and heads for the door. Colin walks behind her, taps her on the shoulder, hands Brooklin her shoes and says, "I think you might need these." Brooklin grabs her shoes and they both laugh.

Back in the office, Brooklin finds two notes on her desk. The first note says Taylor was looking for her. The second note says Erica checked the staff records but none listed a blue Mazda as their vehicle. Without that information, Brooklin really doesn't know how to proceed from this point. She thinks to herself – "Well, Brooklin, maybe you should let Detective Ryan handle the case."

Taylor enters Brooklin's office without knocking and says, "I was looking for you earlier." Brooklin looks at her a little confused. Taylor continues, "Normally you let me know when you are leaving the hotel. Now, I guess you only tell Erica."

Brooklin looks at Taylor and says, "I

have no idea what is troubling you. However if my door is closed, please knock before entering my office. And second, you need to watch your tone with me."

With a controlled voice, Taylor says, "I am your assistant. I need to know how to reach you. I don't know what's happening as of late. However, I feel I am being excluded when decisions are being made."

"Taylor, where I go, when I go and who I tell is none of your concern. I will not call you every time I leave the hotel. If you need to reach me, you have my private cell phone number. Taylor, you are an intelligent woman; therefore, I'm certain you understand that I make all the major decisions at Logan Courtyard, and I determine if and when I would like input from others. Now, why were you looking for me? Is there a problem?" Brooklin asks.

"Here is an example of what I mentioned earlier. No one told me that Tom was going to hire Ron, Larry's son."

"Taylor, before leaving today, I called you on your cell phone informing you that Tom was interested in hiring Ron temporarily. I asked you to talk to Tom and make certain it is a smooth transition."

Taylor takes her cell phone off her belt loop and apparently sees the missed call. She says, "I looked at my cell phone earlier. I don't know how I didn't see that call from you."

"Taylor, do not come in my office and address me in this manner again. You are bordering on disrespect. And I will not tolerate it."

Taylor turns and leaves without an apology. Brooklin shakes her head and thinks, "What is going on with her?"

The front desk informs Brooklin that her 7:00pm appointment is here and Brooklin asks for the young lady to be directed to her office. As Brooklin interviews Karla, there is an instant connection. She really likes Karla. She is professional, sharp and possesses excellent skills. Brooklin tells Karla at the end of the interview that Jill will contact her in the next few days regarding the position. The front desk sends the second candidate who has great skills as well. However, Brooklin was more impressed with Karla. She ends the interview after about twenty minutes and thanks the candidate for her interest in Logan Courtyard.

As Brooklin is clearing her desk for the night, she thinks she hears water dripping in her private bathroom. Her office has a dressing room which includes a floor length mirror, a chaise and a full bathroom with an enclosed shower. Brooklin turns off the water and returns to her office as the phone begins to ring. It's Mark, Larry's brother. He tells her that Larry opened his eyes and the doctor is running tests on him now. Mark says, "He's not talking, but he is awake." Brooklin can hear the excitement in his voice. She tells him that she would like to stop by the hospital to see Larry. Mark replies, "I'm not certain when the doctor will allow Larry to have visitors because he is still in the Trauma ICU. However, I'll call you tomorrow after I speak with his doctor."

"Mark, I'm very happy Larry is improving. I will talk to you tomorrow." Brooklin places the phone on the headset wondering what this development will bring. Will Larry be able to provide any information about the hit and run?

Colin is in the home office working when Brooklin arrives. She stands at the door a moment before he realizes she's there. "Oh, hi," he says. "You worked a little late tonight."

"Yes," Brooklin says smiling. "I want to talk to you about Karla, a young lady I interviewed tonight. She made such an impression on me. She has excellent administrative and communication skills. Here's a copy of her resume. I think she would be the perfect secretary for the Teen Center."

"Brooklin, I'm not replacing Lorna. She is a good employee and Lorna knows all aspects of the Center's day-to-day operation. I'm not interested in re-training someone who probably would not be as good on the job, and Lorna is great with the kids. They love her."

"Colin, I didn't say replace Lorna, even though eventually that may happen. Furthermore, you would not have to re-train her. Meghan and Kathy can train Karla in the administrative part of the job and Lorna can train her on the daily procedures. We can explain to Lorna that we are hiring Karla as office help. Subsequently, this will lessen the responsibilities for the hotel staff. Currently, the hotel staff is responsible for much of the Teen's Center workload."

"And then you will fire Lorna after she trains her replacement?" Colin asks.

"Listen, I think Lorna knows something or may have a part in what happened to Larry. And, Colin, this is done all the time."

"Not by me," he says. "Besides, how do you know Lorna knows anything about Larry's accident? Are you basing this on hearing part of a telephone conversation? Brooklin, I'm not going to fire Lorna because you don't like her or she doesn't like you. We are all professionals."

"Colin," Brooklin says.

"No, Brooklin, and I do not want to discuss it anymore. I told you to let Detective Ryan handle Larry's case. Brooklin, I wouldn't ask you to fire someone at Logan Courtyard because I didn't like them or they didn't like me. That's a little childish, don't you think?"

"Childish? Wow, Colin," Brooklin says and hurries out of the office.

As Brooklin undresses and gets in the shower, she thinks about how angry she is with Colin. She really believes Lorna knows more about what happened to Larry than what she is saying. Why did Colin defend Lorna so quickly? The entire conversation with Colin was very upsetting. Brooklin thought they were in this together, a partnership. Colin knows after what happened in her previous job, how important a coalesced team is to her. Brooklin hesitates, thinking, "No, no, I'm not going there. I'm not going to think about it. I've had many discussions with Colin about our business objectives. All I want is simply to build a cohesive team at Logan Courtyard and the Teen Center. And for that he called me "*childish*?" Brooklin finishes showering, dresses for bed, lies in their king-sized bed and welcomes the solitude.

Chapter 8

Brooklin awakes early and dresses quickly. She does not want to talk to Colin this morning. She picks up her bag as Colin says, "You are leaving early this morning."

"Yes," she says and walks toward the door.

"Brooklin, I apologize for my tone with you last night. When I came to bed, you were asleep. Can we talk for a few minutes now?" he asks.

"Colin, I think you said everything last night and I really don't want to continue the conversation this morning," she says as she walks out the bedroom door.

Brooklin calls Jill later in the morning and explains they will not be filling the position she discussed with her at this time. Brooklin tells her she was very impressed with Karla and, if a position opens and Karla is still available, she would be interested in hiring her. Brooklin apologizes and tells Jill she will talk to her soon.

Brooklin's cell phone vibrates and she sees that Laila is calling. "Hi, Laila."

"Hi, Mom, I didn't get to talk to you

this morning before you left."

"I know, honey, I left early. How are you?" Brooklin asks.

"I'm good. Mom, I think I'm going to stay at home again tonight. Julie is spending the night with a friend and Luke is having a couple of guys over."

"That's fine. Is everything okay?" Brooklin asks.

"Yes, I'm kind of enjoying being home. It's peaceful here. I like spending a little time in my old room and with you and Dad. I'll return to the apartment tomorrow. Besides, the food here is good too," she laughs.

Brooklin laughs too and tells her, "It's still your home. You can sleep at home whenever you like. Oh, Laila, is Luke using your car?"

"Yes, his car should be ready today."

"What was wrong with his car?"

"Don't know Mom. He just asked if he could use my car while his was being repaired. Okay, Mom, gotta go. Maggie is giving me a ride to school."

"Have a good day, honey," Brooklin says.

Brooklin takes her usual quick walk

around the hotel and grabs lunch from the restaurant. She's eating her salad in her office when her cell phone vibrates again. It's Colin calling. "Hi, honey," he says. "You wouldn't talk to me this morning, so I'm hoping we can talk now."

"Colin, there is nothing else to say."

"Brooklin, if you're not willing to talk, how will we come to a resolution?"

"Colin, the resolution is, Karla will not be working at the Teen Center. There is nothing else to discuss and I need to return to work."

"I can tell you are still annoyed with me. I'll talk to you at home. Brooklin, I love you," he says. Brooklin places the phone on her desk, tosses what's left of her salad in the garbage can, and lies back on the leather couch with her feet on the coffee table. After about ten minutes, Brooklin returns to her desk saying, "Okay mental health break is over. I need to gather the strength to continue the day and be prepared for what is sure to come."

She receives a call from Mark, who tells her that they have moved Larry out of ICU and into a private room. Mark says

Brooklin can visit Larry for a few minutes today. She thanks Mark for the call, writes down Larry's room number and tells Mark she should arrive at Memorial around 6:00pm.

Brooklin finds Larry's room. She enters and sees that Larry eyes are closed. There are numerous tubes connected to his body. Mark stands next to Larry's bed clasping his hand, "Larry, please continue to fight. Don't slip away. We've lost mom and dad. You are all I have left." Mark begins to cry, "I need you to fight. You are not alone, I'm here with you."

This reminds Brooklin of what occurred in her office building before she resigned. It's been about two years but she still remembers it as though it was yesterday. She also recalls her anguish and grief. She opens the door quietly to leave but Mark turns and suddenly notices her. "Mark, I'm sorry. I didn't intend to intrude."

Mark greets her and motions for her to step out of the room with him. The doctors have told Mark that there is a chance that Larry can make a full recovery. However, coma patients are susceptible to pneumonia and other infections. Therefore, the doctors and nurses are monitoring Larry closely. The doctors also told Mark that Larry will receive physical therapy to prevent long-term muscle damage. Brooklin tells him to try to think positively. He smiles and says, "I'm hoping and praying, but I am not ashamed to say I'm afraid."

Mark looks so tired. Brooklin asks, "Mark, is there anything I can do for you?"

"No," he says. "I'm fine. I'm just praying that Larry's condition stabilizes. His medical circumstance starts to improve and then he takes a turn for the worse. I took a leave of absence from work. I'm here at the hospital with Larry and I'm taking care of his responsibilities at home." Then Mark looks at Brooklin with gratitude and thanks her for continuing to provide Larry with a full salary being that Larry still has a house payment.

They return to Larry's room and Brooklin asks if Larry's had any other visitors. He said Larry's ex-wife, his son, friends and co-workers from the hotel have come to the hospital. However, Brooklin is the first visitor other than Mark whom doctors have allowed to see Larry since he was admitted to the hospital. Mark informs her that if Larry continues to improve, the doctors will allow another visitor. "I think it will be his son, Ron" Mark says. "I wanted to wait until Larry improved before Ron visits him. Ron is having such a difficult time."

Brooklin looks over at Larry. She walks to his bed and says, "Hi, Larry, it's Brooklin from Logan Courtyard. I am glad you are getting better. The Logan Courtyard family has been praying for your recovery." She sits in a chair near the bed and continues to talk to Larry.

Mark interrupts her briefly, saying he's going to the cafeteria and will return in about twenty minutes. "If you are not here when I return Brooklin, I will call you in the next few days."

She tells him she will be here for about twenty more minutes. Although Larry's head is turned away from Brooklin, she continues to update him on the happenings at the hotel. After several minutes, Larry turns his head toward her. Brooklin stops talking and looks at him a little startled. Slowly, Larry opens his eyes. "Larry," she says, "It's Brooklin." He just looks at her and closes his eyes again. She brings her chair a bit closer to the bed and

Larry opens his eyes and tries to talk. "Larry, don't try to talk. You need to save your strength." Larry leans forward, becomes a little anxious and continues to try to talk. "Larry," she says for a second time, "Please do not try to talk. Try to remain calm." He utters something. "Larry, what are you trying to say?" He is getting agitated. "Larry, take your time. Are you trying to tell me who did this to you?"

Larry leans forward again and forms the single word, "Luke."

Brooklin looks at him in horror. "Did you say, Luke?" she asks as her stomach somersaults. Larry cries out Luke's name once more, fixes his eyes on her and returns his head to the pillow. Slowly, Larry closes his eyes again.

Mark walks in the room and Brooklin is shaking. He walks over to her and asks, "Brooklin, what's wrong? Did something happen? Did something happen with Larry?"

"No, Larry is all right. I just have to leave." She composes herself, stands up and tells him, "I will call you."

"Okay, but are you sure you are okay?"

"Yes, I'm fine. I just have something I

have to take care of -- please, keep me informed on Larry's condition." She hesitates and looks at Larry again. His eyes are closed. He looks like he's asleep. She almost collapses as she walks down the corridor, leaning heavily against the wall. A husky, powerfully built man appears before her and asks, "Are you all right, Ms. Covington?"

Brooklin looks at him saying, "Yes, I'm fine." She pauses, walks out of the hospital and to her car.

As Brooklin drives to the hotel, her mind is racing. Larry clearly said Luke's name. He couldn't have meant Luke was driving the car that hit him. Luke doesn't have a blue Mazda. He drives a black Nissan. Then she begins to think, where is Luke's car? Why did his car need to be repaired? She thinks this cannot be happening. The traffic isn't heavy and she arrives at the hotel quickly. As she enters, she hears Max speak, but she does not answer. She looks in the marketing department but Luke is not there. She asks Katie, the second shift desk clerk, if she has seen Luke. Katie says she saw him earlier walking toward Taylor's office. Brooklin turns and walks down the hall. She walks past several staff members but doesn't utter a word. It's like she is in a trance.

Brooklin walks into Taylor's office and it's dark. Her eyes take a minute to adjust. She sees two people on Taylor's couch and hears heavy breathing. There is a man caressing and kissing a woman. "Taylor," Brooklin says.

Luke leaps up and says, "Mom?" Taylor fumbles to get up and begins buttoning her blouse.

Brooklin shouts, "What is going on in here?" Luke tries to explain and Brooklin tells him to go in her office and wait for her.

"But, Mom" he begins.

Brooklin's voice darkens, "Luke, in my office right now." Luke walks out and Brooklin stares at Taylor. She watches as Taylor struggles to give an explanation. Brooklin understands now, the change in Taylor's work ethics, her attitude and the youthful clothing. When Brooklin couldn't bear to listen to another word, she says, "Taylor, you are fired."

"What?" Taylor says, "You can't fire me. You need me."

"That's where you are mistaken, Taylor.

I do *not* need you."

"You are a cold, ungrateful bitch, but you have crossed the wrong person," hissed Taylor. "I managed this hotel when you were learning the hotel business and now you are going to fire me after I have given five years of my life to this hotel."

"Yes, I am firing you, Taylor. I inherited this hotel; however, I've worked relentlessly to become an expert in the hotel business and have made Logan Courtyard a first-class establishment. You say I am cold and mean? Unfortunately, whenever a woman competes on the same level as men, demands results from her employees and is successful then she is labeled 'difficult' and a 'bitch.' Well, I'll be that if it means negotiating deals, being determined, and informing an assistant that it's time to clear out her desk. I am a good employer and one worthy of respect. You and your personal attacks do not define me. I know who I am and I'm comfortable with who I am. Taylor, your mistake is that you relied on your past performance and shall I say present performance to carry you through. You were a good worker; however, that changed.

During the last few months, it appeared as if you were no longer invested in Logan Courtyard. The quality of your work declined and your attitude became appalling. To date, I haven't received projects assigned to you like the Guidelines and Attendance DVD, and now I find you making out in your office with my son. This is outrageous!"

"You will regret this," Taylor replies. "Mark my word, I will make sure you regret this."

"Pack your belongings, Taylor, and get out of my hotel. As for your threats, you can take them with you. If you try to come after me or anyone I care about, you are going to learn how much of a bitch I can be." Brooklin calls Max to Taylor's office, tells him that Taylor is fired, and directs him to help Taylor pack her possessions, confiscate her badge, key card, hotel parking permit and to escort her out of the hotel. Max nods solemnly at Brooklin and then begins to help Taylor box up her things.

Brooklin returns to her office, opens the door and sees that Luke is not there. She accesses the computer and cancels Taylor's hotel credit card. Tomorrow, she will have

Erica continue the process of closing-out Taylor from Logan Courtyard.

A short time later when Taylor walks in her apartment, she finds Luke sitting on her couch. She stops, places the box with all her personal effects from the hotel on the floor, and asks, "What are you doing here? I thought you would be with your mother," she says spitefully.

"What happened after I left?"

"The bitch fired me."

Luke is shocked that his mother fired Taylor and that Taylor called his mother a bitch. "I will talk to her," he says, "we can fix this."

"I doubt it," Taylor replies, "And I'm not sure I want to return to Logan Courtyard. I am tired. I'm think I'm going to get a shower and go to bed early."

"Okay," Luke says. "It's been a long day and I know you haven't eaten since breakfast. So while you shower, I'll order food for us."

Taylor turns to Luke and says maliciously, "I want you to leave. I want you to leave my apartment now."

Luke looks disheartened and says, "Okay, Taylor. I understand your wanting to be alone. I'll talk to you tomorrow." Taylor stops him and tells him to leave her apartment key on the coffee table. Luke opens his mouth to protest, but Taylor quickly says, "It's over Luke. Leave my key on the coffee table."

"Taylor, think about everything we have done, all the steps we have taken to be together. Did we come this far to just give it all up now? I'll give you some space, but I will not give up on our relationship." He places the key on the coffee table as he leaves.

Chapter 9

When Brooklin arrives home, Colin is walking into the family room. She asks him if Laila is home. "No," Colin says, "she returned to her apartment. Why do you ask?" She tells him what happened at the hospital and about the incident with Taylor and Luke at the hotel. His mouth drops open. He's stunned and doesn't say anything for a couple of minutes. He looks at her and finally says, "Unbelievable." Brooklin looks around and asks, "Colin, is there music playing?"

Then, he remembers the candlelit dinner he had prepared for the two of them in the dining room and shakes his head. "The last two days have been just unreal. Brooklin, let's go in the dining room, have a couple of drinks and try to figure out how we are going to handle this situation."

"I could use a couple of drinks right now," Brooklin replies. In the dining room Brooklin is surprised and rendered speechless. The room has a warm and sensual ambiance. Red rose petals cover the off-white linen tablecloth. The table is set for two with gold dinner cover plates. At the heart of the table is a crystal dish filled with hand-dipped, chocolate covered strawberries with a dozen red roses in crystal vases on each side of the strawberries. Tapers and votive candles are lit and placed throughout the room. Soft music is playing. "Colin, it's beautiful – in fact, it's more than beautiful."

"Yes, I guess it's the thought that counts," he says extinguishing the candles and turning off the music.

Luke arrives calling, "Mom, where are you?" Colin and Brooklin return to the family room.

Colin speaks first, "Luke, is Taylor the person you are in a relationship with?"

"How about *were* in a relationship with. Thanks, mother!" Luke pauses then continues. "Mom, I can't believe you fired her. It's not fair. You're being spiteful and vindictive," he says angrily.

"And what are you being?" she asks. "Manipulated?"

"Mom, I can't believe you said that."

"Apparently you can't believe the truth either, even if it's staring you in the face. Taylor is shrewd and conniving. Luke, you need to learn to read people better.

Otherwise, brace yourself for heartache and manipulation. Furthermore, at the hotel we have clearly established boundaries. Personal relationships are not permitted. We do not want to deal with claims of sexual harassment. No one, including my children, is going to tear down what I've worked hard to build. We maintain a professional relationship with staff members at all times. Luke, do you want to continue to work at Logan Courtyard?"

"Yes, of course, Mom."

"Well, do not cross the line again. Respect my management directives. Now, have a seat and let's forget Taylor for the moment. We have another matter to discuss." Brooklin tells Luke about her conversation with Larry at the hospital.

"What?" Luke says incredulously. "Why would Larry say my name?"

"Luke, I have to ask. Did you have anything to do with Larry's accident?"

"Mom, how could you ask that? You know I would never hit Larry or anyone and then leave the scene. That's unthinkable! I had nothing to do with Larry's accident."

"I know you could never do anything

like that. But I had to ask. Well, let's not overreact. Perhaps Larry didn't know what he was saying. He was just coming out of a coma," Brooklin says.

Colin has been silent and quietly observing Luke and asks, "Son, where were you last Monday night around 10/10:30pm when Larry was hit by the car?"

Luke thinks for a minute and says, "That was the day I injured my ankle. I was here for a portion of the evening and then I went to meet Taylor around that time. Taylor can confirm I was with her. Except now, she wants nothing to do with me."

"That was the day you injured your ankle," Brooklin says, repeating Luke's words and assessing the entire situation. "I don't know how I didn't make that connection. I remember you told me in my office that you left the house because you had something to take care of. And now you're saying that what you had to take care of was meeting Taylor?"

"Yes."

"Luke, you were driving? You were on medication."

"I know, Mom, but I was able to drive."

"If you were on meds, you should *not* have been driving. That's considered driving under the influence. Really, Luke? You know better. What time did you meet Taylor?"

"I don't know. It was after 9pm."

"What time did you return home?" Brooklin asks.

"I'm not sure. I didn't look at the clock."

"Your father and I didn't even realize you left the house. Luke, this is a mess. How do you think this looks? You were injured earlier in the day. Then you leave home later that same evening driving after taking medication. And, of course, this happens to be the night that Larry was hit by the car. What was so important that it couldn't wait?" Luke doesn't answer.

"Luke, why did you meet Taylor that night?" asks Colin.

"Taylor called me and said she needed to see me."

"Luke, do you know how that sounds? Brooklin asks. "Taylor has *that* type of hold on you? Luke, think about this: how much does Taylor really care about you? She knew you injured your ankle that day, yet she phones you and asks you to meet her. Luke, please, I know you are smarter than this." Luke says nothing and looks away from his parents' gaze. "Luke, I'm advising you to not tell Taylor that Larry mentioned your name at the hospital. It's better not to mention any of this to her at this time. Taylor may want revenge and use it against you. She threatened me and said she will make certain I regret firing her."

Colin seemed to be in deep thought, listening intently, and asks, "Luke, where is your car?"

"It's outside, Dad."

Luke realizes he had repair work done and explains, "One of my friends from high school opened an auto repair shop. He replaced my alternator. Dad, you don't think I had anything to do with Larry's accident, do you?"

"It doesn't look good that even though you were injured, you were driving that night while on medication. Larry mentions your name after coming out of a coma. In addition, you had repair work done on your car around the same time period. You didn't take your car to a dealer. You took it to a friend. Luke, do you understand that to anyone looking at this case, this scenario appears suspicious? Is this the first time you've had your car repaired by someone other than the car dealership?" Colin asks.

"Yes, Dad except it was auto repair, not auto body work. And my friend Jamie just opened his repair shop this month. Does anyone know what kind of car hit Larry? It wasn't my car. I know how things look, I'm not naïve. But I didn't have anything to do with Larry's accident. Dad, don't you believe me?"

There is an awkward silence. Colin doesn't respond. "Okay, let's slow down. As I said earlier, Larry is just coming out of a coma," Brooklin pauses for a moment. "I wasn't certain if I should even mention this until I talk to Larry again. But then, I thought you and your father should be aware of what was said. I will call Mark tomorrow and try to gain as much information as possible. Afterwards, I'll call both of you and tell you what I learned. This almost certainly will not develop into anything. Therefore, it's better to keep this quiet and not discuss it with anyone," Brooklin says.

"Mom, thanks for believing in me."

"Luke, try not to worry. You can be certain your father and I will stand by you and we will work through this together as a family."

"Thanks, Mom," he says, looks briefly at his father with frustration and walks out the door.

Colin is still withdrawn as Brooklin says, "I think Luke was hoping for a little more support from you."

"Brooklin, please. What if Larry gives Luke's name to the detective who is investigating this case? Or to his brother? I had to ask Luke those questions so he can be prepared rather than try to cover up the truth."

"Cover up the truth? Oh now, you're accusing me too. Colin, I'm not trying to cover up anything. I, unlike you, don't believe there is *anything* to cover up. I just think we should not discuss this situation with anyone until we are absolutely clear on all the facts. And Colin, it's okay to ask the questions, but where is your compassion?"

"Brooklin, Luke is a grown man. Apparently, you're not remembering how he spoke to you earlier regarding Taylor?"

"I do remember. Luke being angry with me does not justify my not standing with him when he's in need of support," Brooklin exclaims.

"Support or do you mean *cuddle*?" asks Colin.

Brooklin eyes him with resentment. "Colin, I saw disappointment and hurt on Luke's face. I'm sure he wanted support from his mother and father. Lately you seem to be supporting everyone except your family."

Colin turns to Brooklin and asks, "You want to clarify that statement Brooklin? Are you speaking of Lorna?"

Brooklin is overwhelmed with so many emotions. She walks upstairs and gets dressed for a work out in their home gym. About thirty minutes later, Colin walks into the gym. Brooklin continues on the elliptical. Colin quietly says, "Brooklin, one of the reasons, I love you is because you are a great mother. Our kids and I are fortunate to have you. I apologize for the comment I made earlier. And for the record, nothing or no one is more important than my family. Lately, it seems that I've made a number of inappropriate comments. I've been stressed with the phonathon and the demands at work. However, now I would like to share some appropriate comments coming straight from the heart. Brooklin, I'm blown away by your principles, your loyalty and your beauty inside and outside. I love looking in those gorgeous eyes every day and hearing your enthusiastic laughter."

"Colin, I appreciate all you've said, although I'm unsure which heart those words came from." Brooklin walks toward the door.

"Honey, can we try to revive our evening?"

"Colin, I'm going to take a shower and go to bed. It's been a long, exasperating day." Colin looks at Brooklin as she walks through the door and thinks, okay, she is still heated.

Chapter 10

When Brooklin arrives at work, Ron is working mulch into one of the flower beds. They exchange "good mornings" and Brooklin asks, "How is everything?"

"Everything is fine," Ron answers. Then with a little uncertainty he adds, "I want to thank you again for the job, Ms. Covington."

"I hear you are doing great, Ron, and we are happy to have you at Logan Courtyard. I checked on your father's condition yesterday and am happy to know he's improving."

"Yes, I've heard," he says.

"Okay, Ron, you have a good day." Brooklin walks through the side entrance near her office and finds a large bouquet of flowers on her desk. The card reads: *"I absolutely love and admire you. Colin"*

Erica walks in and immediately comments on the flowers. Then she says, "Brooklin, I heard that you fired Taylor last night. What happened?"

Brooklin answers, "Taylor's conduct was unacceptable."

"No one liked her anyway. The staff is

glad you fired her," says Erica. "Everyone is saying she was being her normal, rude self and you fired her."

"Is that all you heard?"

"That's all that's being said, as far as I know. Is there more?" she asks.

"I was just wondering. The rumor mill always adds more," Brooklin says.

"Not this time, I guess," replies Erica. "As I said, everyone is happy she's gone. Max brought in Taylor's badge, key card and hotel parking permit and when I closed Taylor out as a company employee, I noticed that you had canceled her credit card."

"Yes, I did. Erica, would you have Jeff come down to meet with me in the next hour? I am certain we need to change several of Logan Courtyard's passwords. I also want to know what other safeguards we need to have in place now that Taylor's no longer an employee."

"I'll call Jeff as soon as I return to my desk. Do you want me to call Jill as well to have her send candidates to replace Taylor?"

"No, I'll work alone for now."

"Isn't that too much work for one person?"

"I'll be fine."

"Well, Brooklin, I'll help you as much as I can."

"Thanks, Erica. I guess I better get to work since I don't have an assistant." Erica smiles and returns to her desk humming.

After meeting with Jeff, Brooklin works about an hour before her mind returns to Larry's case. She makes the decision to take a quick break and phone Detective Ryan. "Ms. Covington, it's nice to hear from you. Did you miss me?" She ignores his question and asks him if he can meet with her tomorrow morning regarding Larry's case.

"I can be in your office around 10am."

"That will be fine, Detective Ryan. I'll see you tomorrow." She makes a mental note of what she needs to discuss with the detective and then returns to the tasks before her.

About mid-day, Brooklin telephones Mark. "Hi, Brooklin. How are you today?" Mark asks.

"I'm fine, Mark. How are you?"

"I'm doing well. Larry's condition is about the same. The doctors say he is progressing as expected. Thank you again for coming to the hospital yesterday."

"Well, I appreciate you allowing me to visit Larry. Is he talking or responding to conversation yet?"

"No, he's not talking. The doctors say that sometimes those who emerge from a coma survive with a brain that may be different. There can be mental and physical problems, or they can make a full recovery. I'm hoping Larry will rest, regain his strength and recover completely," Mark says. "He did open his eyes a few times today."

"Mark, please continue to keep me informed of his condition."

Brooklin calls Colin and updates him on Larry's condition and thanks him for the flowers. She then calls Luke, provides the same information and inquires about his state of mind today.

"Mom, I'm fine. I'm not scheduled to work this afternoon, I decided to take the day off from school too. I just need a day to clear my head. I'll return to my normal routine tomorrow."

"Okay, Luke, I'll talk to you tomorrow."

Luke calls Taylor a second time after

talking to his mother. Again, there's no answer. "Taylor, I've called you a couple of times today. Can you pick up the phone?" He hesitates for a moment. "Okay, Taylor, can you please return my call? I didn't go to class, so you can call me at any time." Luke knows Taylor is not going to return his call. It's over and he needs to accept it. He takes a shower and puts on a t-shirt with his pajama bottom. He looks in the refrigerator, decides to heat yesterday's pizza and returns to the couch. After taking a bite of the pizza, he changes the television channels until he comes to the "Detective Story" marathon. "Today I watch marathons and tomorrow I have to move forward," Luke says. He thinks how he regrets getting soft and letting down his guard. "Thanks, Taylor, for the lesson," he says at the top of his voice and takes another bite of pizza.

   Brooklin walks into the restaurant and asks Will for a cup of coffee. "A cup of coffee coming up! Light and sweet, right?" says Will. "Ms. Brooklin, you're working late tonight." Brooklin looks up at the clock. It's 10pm. Wow, she thinks, she still has another couple of hours to work before going home. "What happened to Larry is real sad," Will remarks. "Do you think he'll be able to return to work?"

"I hope he will be able to return."

"Yeah, it's just real sad," Will repeats. She thanks Will for the coffee and returns to her office feeling re-energized. She hears her telephone ringing.

It's Colin. "Brooklin, you're still at work? When are you coming home?"

"I have a couple more hours of work."

"Can't whatever you are doing wait until tomorrow?"

"No, Colin, it can't. Remember, I don't have an assistant. I have to finish this work tonight. Why don't you come down to the hotel? Or we could meet at El Chateau in a couple of hours for drinks?" she asks. He begins to argue. "Colin, I'm not going to argue with you. The sooner I finish this work, the sooner I can leave the hotel."

"Fine," he says and Brooklin hears a click. She returns to work.

When she enters their bedroom, the clock says 12:18am. Colin is asleep. In the bathroom, she lights some candles and runs bath water. Restless and wide awake, she lies back in the tub, closes her eyes and listens to some soft, mellow music. There's nothing like the simple pleasure of a warm bath. The cares of the day seem to fade away. Finally, she relaxes and begins to doze. She compels herself to move from the tub and into bed.

Chapter 11

Brooklin arrives at work the next morning and practically everyone has a question. She welcomes the demands of the day given it deters thoughts of anything other than work. A few minutes before 10, Detective Ryan walks in wearing his typical sports jacket and jeans. "Good morning, Ms. Covington."

"Good morning, Detective." Erica brings them coffee and they sit at the round table at the far corner of her office. "Detective, anything yet regarding the hit and run?"

"I'm still investigating the case."

"Come on, Detective, how is the case going?"

"Ms. Covington, I can't discuss our investigation. However I will tell you, all our information up to this point remains inconclusive."

"I heard you guys are stumped," Brooklin says with a coy smile.

"You hear a lot of things, don't you?" he says returning the smile. Then he continues, "This is a difficult case."

"Well," Brooklin says, "I think I can help. I understand that Larry was quite the ladies' man including being involved with married women. Maybe, his past caught up with him. Perhaps, a husband wanting to settle the score?"

The detective smiles, "Yes, I've heard about the affairs from several different sources." He takes notes as Brooklin tells him about both the discussion she heard between Linda and Lorna and her conversation with Jerry. Afterwards, Brooklin calls Erica asking her to set up meetings for Detective Ryan to question Linda, Lorna and Jerry. As Brooklin places the telephone on the headset, Detective Ryan looks at her and quickly scribbles something on his notepad and passes it to her. The note reads: "I think your office is bugged. Just agree with whatever I say." Brooklin looks at him confused. "Ms. Covington, can we finish this conversation in the restaurant? I'd like to grab a bagel before I question your staff," he says and motions for her to say yes. "Of course," Brooklin says and they walk out of her office, past Erica's desk, through the double doors and down the hall. Then

Detective Ryan repeats, "I really think your office is bugged."

"What?" Brooklin exclaims. "Bugged?"

"Yes, and if I'm right, I needed you to leave your office without the person responsible becoming suspicious. I heard sounds coming from your phone headset. Noise coming from a headset when it's hung up can be caused by a hook switch bypass which turns the telephone receiver into an eavesdropping microphone and also a speaker. Somebody could be listening to everything you say or do within twenty feet of the phone. I'm calling the squad room to have a couple of our guys sweep your offices and the conference rooms." Brooklin looks at him horrified.

Brooklin sits in the VIP section of the bar and watches Detective Ryan have a discussion with two plain-clothes officers and then lead them to her office. He returns after about ten minutes and tells Brooklin that he had advised Erica in writing that a technical security inspection is being conducted and that she should not discuss it with anyone. Brooklin is concerned and asks, "What's your take on all of this?"

"Ms. Covington," he says, "this case is becoming more complicated by the day. With your permission, I'd like to set up a work area in one of the conference rooms until this case is solved."

"All right, but with one condition." He raises his eyebrows and looks at her questioningly.

"I would like to work the case with you. I want to find the person who bugged my office."

"It's not a good idea for civilians to try to help with an investigation."

"Well, let's not say, I'm helping with the investigation. Let's say I'm providing you with leads and you are informing me of certain outcomes."

He looks down at her and smiles, "That would mean we would have to spend a great deal of time together." She looks at him suspiciously. "However, if you are not up to it," he says.

"No, I'm up to it." Brooklin says.

Brooklin sits through a marketing presentation in Meeting Room One trying to focus on what is being said and not the distraction of the police sweep in their offices. Erica is the only staff member aware of what's currently taking place. Detective Ryan had informed Brooklin that it will take between two to six hours for the recording devices' search to be completed. Therefore, Erica and Brooklin decided to work in one of the suites upstairs and Detective Ryan was assigned to a suite as well. Then Brooklin remembers. She must phone Agent Dalton and inform him of the possibility of a bug in her office. She wonders if having that Mr. Reed from the witness protection program has anything to do with the bug.

After her meeting, she walks upstairs, places her key card in the door inscribed 207 and enters the suite. Erica's in the front room working on the computer. Brooklin walks into the bedroom, places her paperwork on the desk and closes the door. She telephones Agent Dalton and tells him of the possibility of a listening device on her office telephone. He asks for the name of the precinct where Detective Ryan works. She provides him with the information and he tells Brooklin he will call her Monday.

Brooklin telephones Colin. In all the

commotion, she forgot to call Colin and tell him what had occurred. She relays the details of the day and he is astonished. "Brooklin, are you okay? I can be there in about twenty minutes."

"Colin, I'm fine. There's no need for you to come. I have a great deal of work to finish before I come home this evening. I'll just see you at home tonight."

"Well, if you are certain you are okay. Brooklin, please don't work too late tonight."

Detective Ryan stops by the suite and tells Brooklin that he plans to question the three staff members in a few minutes. However, he wants to let her know that there *was* indeed a listening device on her phone and asks her if she had any idea who might be responsible. "No, I can't think of anyone or when someone would have had an opportunity." Brooklin does not mention that the bug may have something to do with the FBI taking up residence on the eleventh floor of Logan Courtyard. "I did terminate three employees recently. However, I really don't think they would bug my office, and they were escorted out of the hotel after being terminated. Besides, we have security staff and surveillance cameras in the hotel.

"All right," replies the detective, "I would like you to give me the name, address and telephone number of the three employees who were terminated. And I would like you to continue to give this some thought. Keep in mind, there was a bug placed on your telephone. The officers are currently doing an electronic enhanced search of the walls, ceilings, floors and a physical examination of interior and exterior areas in your offices and conference rooms. The officers and I will stop back after they have completed the job."

"Thanks for everything," Brooklin says.

"You do not have to thank me. I'm just glad we found the bug," he says. "And before you ask me, I want you to know that I'm going to try to keep this quiet. I'll talk to the two officers, the sergeant and my lieutenant. I can't guarantee it but, as always, I will do my best to keep this news from reaching the media."

"Thank you," Brooklin says again. She makes a mental note to prepare a press release just in case.

Brooklin hears Detective Ryan ask Erica to schedule Linda as his first appointment followed by Lorna and finally Jerry. The detective mentioned he specifically wanted Lorna to know that Linda had been questioned first but to be unclear about what Linda revealed during the questioning.

Linda walks into Suite 209 looking a little uneasy. Detective Ryan greets her and asks her to have a seat. "Ms. Johnson, I have a few more questions for you regarding Larry Carter's case."

"Okay."

"Ms. Johnson, when I last spoke to you, you told me you were not aware of Mr. Carter being in a relationship or dating anyone. Is that correct?"

She looks at him and answers, "Yes, that is correct."

"Ms. Johnson, my question for you today is, are you aware of any of Mr. Carter's prior relationships other than his ex-wife?"

She hesitates and then says, "No, I'm not."

"Ms. Johnson, I have heard otherwise. Therefore, would you like to rethink that answer?" He is assuming that Linda or Lorna had some type of relationship with Larry Carter. Now, hopefully this strategy works.

She looks at him and says softly, "Lorna Young told me she dated Larry. I don't know if they were in a relationship."

"How long did Mr. Carter and Ms. Young date?"

"I'm not sure. I think probably, about a month."

"When and why did the relationship end?"

"It ended about a month before the accident. I'm not sure why Lorna stopped seeing Larry. She only said that he was not the man for her."

"She didn't give any other explanation? Was she angry with him?"

She looks at the detective, then looks away and says, "No, she was not angry with him. She just stopped taking his calls."

"Ms. Johnson, does Lorna or anyone you know drive a blue Mazda?"

She thinks for a minute and then answers, "No."

"Ms. Johnson, have you heard or are you aware of any information regarding who was driving the car that hit Mr. Carter?"

"No. I have told you all I know."

"Ms. Johnson, are you certain you have told me all you know about this case?"

She nods and says, "Yes, I really have. I do not know any more about Larry or his accident."

"All right, Ms. Johnson, thank you for your time. If you remember or hear any information regarding this case, please let me know. I will be using Conference Room One here at the hotel as my office until this case is solved." As Linda leaves the room, it is clear that she notices Lorna waiting to be questioned. Lorna observes Linda as she exits and is visibly troubled about what Linda might have told Detective Ryan.

"Ms. Young," Detective Ryan says smiling, "come in." Lorna looks very serious as she walks in. Detective Ryan waves his hand in the direction of the chair and says, "Please have a seat. I have a few more questions for you regarding Larry Carter's hit and run case." Lorna nods. "Ms. Young, when I last spoke to you, you told me you were not aware of any past or present relationships of Mr. Carter other than his ex-wife. Is that correct?" She merely looks at him. "Ms. Young, is this correct?"

"Yes," she answers.

"Ms. Young, would you like to change your answer at this time?" She doesn't answer. "Ms. Young, were you involved or did you have a relationship with Mr. Carter?"

She breathes loudly and says, "Yes."

"What type of relationship did you have with Mr. Carter?"

She says dryly, "We dated."

"Did you have a sexual relationship with him?"

"Yes," she says frowning.

"How long did the relationship last?"

"It was very brief, about a month."

"When did it end?"

"I ended the relationship about two months ago."

"How did you end the relationship?"

"Larry phoned me and I told him I didn't think we should see each other anymore. Then I stopped answering his calls."

"You didn't tell him why?"

"I grew tired of his continual calls, and the last time he called I told him I wasn't interested in dating him any longer. I

146

explained that I heard some disturbing things about him."

"What did you hear about him?"

"I really do not want to discuss it. It has nothing to do with this case."

"How do you know there isn't a connection to the case? What did you hear about Mr. Carter?"

She fiddles with some tissue in her hands and says angrily, "He gambles. Apparently, Larry was heavily in debt. He was about to lose his house and he borrowed money from some shady people."

"Gambling?" Detective Ryan repeats. "Did you ask him if this was true?"

"No, after I mentioned the disturbing news, there was silence. I took the silence as guilt."

"You stopped dating Larry because he gambled?"

"I was disgusted. I don't need criminals coming after me because of Larry.

"Ms. Young, who told you Mr. Carter gambled and borrowed money?"

"John, a friend, told me."

"And you believe John?"

"Yes, he's a good friend and would not

lie to me. Besides, now I'm hearing rumors that these goons were driving the car that hit Larry."

"Have you heard what type of car hit Larry?"

"No, I haven't heard anything about the type of car."

"Can you write down for me John's full name, address and telephone number?" Lorna provides Detective Ryan with the information. "Ms. Young, do you know anyone else Mr. Carter may have had a relationship with or been involved with?"

"No."

"Do you know anyone who drives a blue Mazda?"

"No," she answers.

"Ms. Young, have you heard who loaned Mr. Carter money or who was driving the car that hit Mr. Carter?"

"No, I haven't."

"Ms. Young, do you know any other details regarding Mr. Carter or his accident that we have not discussed? I want you to think before you answer and then respond truthfully. I do not want to have to arrest you for obstruction of justice."

"Obstruction of justice? How can you arrest me for obstruction?"

"How about for misleading and providing false information to a police officer?"

Looking nervous, Ms. Young says, "Truthfully, I have told you all I know."

"Okay, Ms. Young, if you remember or hear any information regarding this case, let me know. I will be using Conference Room One here at the hotel as my office until this case is solved."

Minutes later, Jerry knocks on the door and says, "You wanted to see me?"

"Yes. I have a few more questions for you regarding Larry Carter's hit and run case. Mr. Cole, since last we talked, have you heard or learned any additional information regarding Mr. Carter's case?"

"No, sir," Jerry says.

"Do you know of any habits, addictions or activities Mr. Carter may have been involved in?"

"No, sir."

"Have you heard about any relationships Larry may have had with any women other than his ex-wife?"

"No, sir."

"Has anyone mentioned why Larry was hit by a car or who may have hit him?"

"No, sir. I haven't heard anything."

Detective Ryan laughs and says, "Mr. Cole, are you trying to play me? I think you know more than you're telling me."

"No, sir, I don't know anything about this case."

"Well, Mr. Cole, I actually know a little about you. I did my homework. I know after you get your paycheck on Fridays, you meet a friend around 7pm on the corner of Jay and Liberty Streets. I think I have a picture of a transaction occurring on that corner."

"No, sir. I haven't made any transactions. I'm innocent."

Detective Ryan laughs again and says, "Really, you don't look like a guy who is innocent. Maybe, we should take a ride to the station, you and I, and take a closer look at that picture. I'm certain you are in that photo."

"Better to be in jail than dead," Jerry says shrugging his shoulders.

"Okay, Jerry. Then, jail it is."

"Sir, hold up, hold up for a minute. I

think I do recall hearing that Larry slept with a lot of women and that he gambled a lot."

"Is that all you heard?"

"I heard that he owed money to some dangerous people and they put a hit on him."

"The dangerous people being whom, exactly?"

"Sir, I don't know."

"Well, I guess we are going to have to take that ride to the precinct."

Jerry begins to sweat. "Look, this is just between you and me, right? I don't need these people coming after me." He is panicking.

"Mr. Cole, take it easy. This is just between you and me. Now, who are the people?"

"I'm not sure, but it's probably Big Mel. Guys normally borrow money from Big Mel, and Mel may alter parts of their body if they don't pay on time. If you know what I mean?"

"Where can I find Big Mel?"

"He hangs down at The Pit on 5th. Sir, this is just between us, right?"

"Right, Mr. Cole. However, I advise you to get clean and stop hanging on the corner of Jay and Liberty Streets. The next time we see you there, you'll be taken to the station and booked."

Jerry says anxiously, "You don't have to say it twice. I will definitely not be hanging on *any* street corners again." He looks relieved and says, "Sir, is there anything else I can do to help?"

"Mr. Cole, do you know anyone who drives a blue Mazda?"

"No, I don't think I know anyone who drives a blue Mazda."

"Okay, if you remember or hear any information regarding this case, please let me know. I will be using Conference Room One here at the hotel as my office until this case is solved."

"You mean you're going to stay here at the hotel until you all solve the case?

"Yes, I am."

"Well, what happens if you don't solve the case?"

"I guess Logan Courtyard will have a permanent guest. So, stay clean and if you hear anything, let me know. The faster the case is solved, the faster I can return to the precinct."

Jerry smiles as he leaves and says, "Yes, sir."

It's about 6:00pm, when Detective Ryan returns to the suite. He informs Brooklin that the two officers will arrive in the suite shortly. Erica has left for the day and Brooklin is working on the computer in the front room. She welcomes a quick break. The officers enter the suite and report that no other listening devices were found. Detective Ryan tells the two officers he wants them to perform a second sweep in a couple of weeks. They inform Brooklin of some preventive practices and she thanks them again.

Brooklin looks at Detective Ryan and says, "So, what have you learned?"

"First, I would like you to know that I questioned your security staff again today. This weekend, I will begin checking the surveillance tapes." He sat down and briefed her on his conversations with the three employees.

She looks at him and says, "Talk about gathering information! What are your thoughts on all this?" she asks.

"My thoughts are that I have some investigative work ahead of me," he says simply.

"Well, if all this is true, I guess Larry was not a happy man. He was dealing with some pain of his own," she says.

"Why do you say that?"

She thinks about all she has heard about Larry and asks Detective Ryan, "What are your views on why people cheat?"

He looks at her and says, "Maybe because they are unhappy at home? Why do you think people cheat?"

"I think some may not be happy at home. But I also think some people cheat because they have low self-esteem and carry some baggage from the past. Like those who felt unpopular, not well-liked, who were mistreated or were not accepted during their childhood or teen years. Cheating in their later years gives them some false sense of self-worth."

"It seems like you have given this a lot of thought," he says.

"I know women who stay with men who cheat. They continue to make sacrifices and give of themselves until their self-esteem reaches a low level. It's the blind leading the blind, indicative of a mutual lack of the essential ingredient, self-love."

Detective Ryan fixes his eyes on her and says, "It could just be that they are not happy at home."

Brooklin looks at him and continues, "What the person being cheated on fails to realize is that the cheating has nothing to do with them. The deficiency lies in the cheater. It's as if the cheater feels he is being validated by this behavior. In any case, that's what I think. If Larry cheats and gambles, I think there is definitely a character flaw. Anyway to return to Larry's case, what's next?" she asks.

Detective Ryan says, "Monday, I visit Larry at Memorial." Brooklin swallows. Suddenly, it feels like a current of cold, blustery wind is blowing through the room. She recovers quickly realizing she is with one of the best detectives in the area. Brooklin begins mulling over what Larry will tell Detective Ryan. Suddenly, she decides to bring her work day to a close.

"Detective Ryan, I am going home for the evening."

"All right, Ms. Covington, I need to return to the precinct and then I'll be going home too. I know tomorrow is Saturday. But do you plan to be at the hotel tomorrow?" he asks.

"I'll be at the Teen Center all day tomorrow. However, I plan to stop at the hotel for a couple of hours tomorrow evening," she says.

"We'll talk tomorrow evening then," Detective Ryan says. "Listen, since we're working together and both have a stake in this case, can we become less formal and use first names?" he asks.

"I think that would be okay," she replies.

Detective Ryan walks Brooklin to her car and says, "Good night, Brooklin."

"Good night," Brooklin says as she starts her drive home, thinking, what a day.

Chapter 12

As Brooklin enters the family room, Colin calls out, "You're home? Good, would you like a glass of wine?"

"No, thanks," Brooklin says and sits at the opposite end of the couch.

"Brooklin, are things that bad between us that you can't sit next to me on the sectional?" He rubs his hand over the cushion and says, "There is all this empty space. You know, that's how the house feels when you're not here. It's this huge empty space." Colin moves over next to Brooklin and takes her hand saying, "Brooklin, I miss you."

She looks at him and then looks down, "Colin, I know I work long hours most nights, but this will not last forever. We agreed I would devote this time to the hotel. Colin, if you miss me, why don't you come to the hotel. We can have dinner or you can be part of the effort and work some hours at the hotel."

"Brooklin, that's your baby. I'm not interested in working at the hotel."

"Okay, I guess you're not interested in having dinner with me unless, of course, it's

on your terms. Colin, I am totally drained.
I'm actually glad I told you earlier about the
bug in my office because I do not have the
energy to focus on it now."

"So, there *was* a bug placed on your
telephone?"

"Yes, there was."

"Do you have any idea of who planted
the bug?"

"No, Colin, I don't. The good news is
Detective Ryan has decided he will use one of
the conference rooms at the hotel as an office
until Larry's case is solved."

Colin looks at Brooklin and says,
"That's unusual."

"Unusual or not, I'm glad he'll be at the
hotel," she answers. "I'm going to shower
and go to bed. Can we continue this
conversation tomorrow morning?"

"Sure," Colin says sounding a little
cold.

"Good night, Colin," Brooklin says and
walks upstairs.

The next morning when Colin comes
downstairs, Brooklin's at the kitchen table
reading the paper and having a cup of coffee.
"Good morning," he says.

"Good morning. I baked muffins. Would you like one?" Brooklin asks pointing to the muffins on the table. Colin takes a muffin, pours himself a cup of coffee and sits at the table. "How is work at the Teen Center?"

"Everything is going well," he smiles and adds, "Your brother Jim is doing a good job. He and the kids are always joking and laughing. There's a mutual respect between them. He's at work every day and on time. He's a great addition to the Teen Center."

"That's absolutely wonderful. Maybe he's found his calling. I'll call him later and congratulate him on a good job."

"Jim's working at the Teen Center today, so you don't have to call him."

"Sounds good. It will be nice to see Jim." Brooklin looks at Colin and says, "Detective Ryan is going to the hospital to question Larry Monday morning and I'm not sure what Larry is going to tell him."

"Well, Brooklin, we can't worry about it. We have to just wait for the outcome. Luke needs to learn that actions have consequences."

"What are you insinuating? Colin, say

what's on your mind. Are you accusing Luke?"

"Of course not."

"Then, what are you saying?" Brooklin pauses a moment. "You know, Colin, I can't pretend I'm not a little displeased with your temperament lately. I really don't know what is happening with us. Normally, we're able to have conversations. Now, it seems our discussions turn into an argument or end with your being abrupt with me."

"I know. Brooklin, the truth is I miss the Brooklin I married." She looks at him confused. "Brooklin, before you inherited the hotel you worked, but during the evenings you were home taking care of me and the kids. Now, it's like you have another baby."

"Colin, in the past, I managed everything -- the kids, the household, my career and made sure your needs were met. I never complained about you working long hours or your time away from home. My mother died and I inherited the hotel. I've worked hard to generate success for the hotel and for me. If you or the kids need me, I'm there. My family comes first. However, now the kids are older and out of the house."

"Yes, Brooklin. But I'm here. I'm retired and missing you."

"Colin, I hear you. Can we come to some type of compromise? Presently, I have this responsibility of the hotel and it requires my attention. I love my work at the hotel. I feel it's finally my time. The time is right for me to seize this moment to improve and create new business and staff the hotel with the right mix of talented and creative people. I can't go back or become paralyzed now, not even for you. Can you stand by me?"

"Well," he says as he stands and begins to walk away. "I guess I can read between the lines."

"What does that mean? Colin, you made your choices. You retired and I thought you were enjoying your retirement. You're playing golf and working at the Teen Center. These are all your decisions. I really have tried to balance my responsibilities at work with commitment to the family."

He continues walking. "Colin." He doesn't answer and disappears through the kitchen door. Brooklin sits at the table for a few minutes and then decides to go for a run to clear her head.

Brooklin returns to the house after a thirty minute run. Colin is dressed and looks at her as she reaches for a cold bottle of water. "Where were you?"

"Running. I wanted to begin my work day with a quiet, peaceful mind."

He places his coffee cup in the dishwasher and says, "I have an appointment with my barber in a few minutes. I'll see you at the Teen Center later."

"Okay," Brooklin says.

After Brooklin showers, she walks in her closet. She chooses casual and relaxed clothing -- a t-shirt, blue jeans and sneakers. It actually feels good. In her car, she puts the top down on her SLK Mercedes convertible and welcomes the sun and the gentle breeze. As the smooth and mellow cd plays, she blocks out the noise in her head.

Brooklin is working in her little office at the Teen Center when she hears Jim talking as he enters the center. She walks to her office door and asks him to come in for a few minutes. He looks a little hesitant. Brooklin regrets they do not have a better relationship. However, she couldn't close her eyes to his poor work performance and behavior at the hotel. "Jim," Brooklin smiles and says, "so how is everything?"

"Fine."

"Colin tells me you are doing an excellent job here at the Teen Center. I would like to thank you and commend you on a job well done."

"This is a surprise," he says.

"Well, we appreciate the work you are doing and I'm sure the kids are grateful for you as well. Okay, I won't keep you from your duties. You take care and I'll talk to you soon."

Brooklin works until about 3:00pm. She stops briefly at Colin's office to let him know she's leaving for the day.

"Brooklin, we didn't discuss the listening device found on your office phone at the hotel. Do you have any idea who may have placed it there?"

"No, I don't. I'm baffled about this situation."

"Brooklin, this is serious. I think I need to have a conversation with Logan Courtyard security. I want to make certain that there are safety measures in place for you."

"Well, Detective Ryan is investigating and doesn't want staff members told a device was found in my office at this time."

"Are you headed home?" he asks.

"No. I'm meeting Jill for dinner and then I'm going to stop at the hotel for a couple of hours. After that, I'll be home. What about you?" she asks.

"I'm leaving here in a few minutes. I'm going to play 9 holes and then, home. I guess, I'll see you around 7:30?" he asks.

"Yes, I'll be home around 7:30," Brooklin says.

Jill and Brooklin meet at their favorite restaurant, Talb, a popular gathering place for locals and visitors. Talb offers great food, friendly and efficient service and it's down the street from the Teen Center and Logan Courtyard. Brooklin arrives at the table where Jill is seated. Jill is a petite woman with a beautiful smile and a beautiful heart to match. She reminds Brooklin of the girl next door. Brooklin looks forward to their talks. Jill is married to Levy, Colin's and Brooklin's lawyer for the Teen Center and Logan Courtyard. As Brooklin settles in the booth, the waiter comes and takes their order. "So how are you?" Jill asks. "You look stressed."

"I'm fine. I'm just dealing with several problems at the moment." Their waiter returns with their salads and wine. "How about you?" Brooklin asks.

"I'm fine," Jill says. Business is a little slow, therefore I'm thinking of doing a little advertising. Before I make any decisions, I'd like your opinion. I really trust and value your business advice," she says.

"Sure, I would love to help."

"Okay, now tell me what's going on," Jill says.

Brooklin brings her up-to-date on Colin's and her relationship, Detective Ryan and explains that Larry's hit and run case is still not solved. Brooklin decides not to provide any details regarding Larry's case, his mentioning Luke's name, or the bug found in her office. Brooklin just doesn't feel comfortable talking about this information at this time. And she definitely can't mention Logan Courtyard's special guests. Jill asks, "You and Colin are not connecting these days?"

"No. Colin and my relationship has

always been easy and interesting. Now, it's just exhausting. I still love him. I just think he is so self-centered. When he worked long hours, I never nagged him. When I inherited the hotel, I explained to Colin I would need about a year and a half to two years to transform Logan Courtyard. Jill, I inherited a quality hotel but I wanted Logan Courtyard to be superior, to be one of the finest."

"Were the two of you in agreement?"

"Yes, but Colin has chosen to change the rules and forfeit the agreement. I expressed to Colin how important it was for me to have an exceptional hotel with an exceptional group of employees who work well together. I know staff members will not always agree, but I want to create a team that will respect their colleagues."

"Do you think you need to talk to Colin about where you are on this timeline?"

"Yes, Jill, I do. I need at least a few more months for this to materialize, allowing me to feel comfortable relinquishing some of my responsibilities. I inherited the hotel and 85% of its staff. I need to know my management staff and I are on the same page, and I must have a certain level of confidence in them to delegate certain duties. I'm not there yet."

"Brooklin, be honest, will you ever feel comfortable?"

"Yes, I can honestly say I can and will. In the interim, I'll continue to work on balancing my marriage, family and work. Hopefully, Colin will too and we can move through this."

"Now, what is Detective Ryan like?"

"Detective Ryan is one of the best detectives in the area. He's handsome, amusing, clever and intelligent."

"Brooklin, are you attracted to him?"

"No." She pauses a second and adds, "well a little. But, I will not allow any lines to be crossed."

"You may not but will he make attempts? If he does, it may become a struggle for you -- blurred lines?"

Brooklin looks a little uneasy and says, "We are just friends, that's all."

"You know what they say, men and women cannot be just friends."

"Okay, we'll just be business associates. Now, will you stop? You know how I feel about cheating."

Brooklin can see from the expression on Jill's face, that she too is thinking about their friend Lydia. They both still feel the pain of losing her. Brooklin had met Lydia in the workplace. Brooklin introduced her to Jill and the three of them enjoyed a great friendship. Lydia became involved with their supervisor. They both were single. Unfortunately, he cheated on Lydia continuously and even began to treat her badly in the workplace. Jill and Brooklin talked to Lydia about transferring to another department or finding other employment. Lydia remained at the job and was ridiculed by other employees. Of course, the employees did not talk about Lydia to her face, although Lydia knew she was the topic in many conversations. As a supervisor, Brooklin walked a fine line of being supportive of Lydia and remaining professional and fair to all the employees. One morning, Brooklin arrived to work late due to a doctor's appointment. She heard a couple of the employees laughing and saying he finally dumped her. She is so pathetic. Brooklin walked down to Lydia's office and found her lying on the floor near the couch in her office, unresponsive and lifeless. Brooklin screamed for help, for someone to call 911. She tried to revive Lydia, but she couldn't. Lydia committed suicide in her office by overdosing on pills. She took her own life over a man who was not even worthy of her. She loved this man more than she loved herself. Brooklin resigned from her job. She never returned. It's something she will never forget. Jill and Brooklin look at each other with tears in their eyes. Jill grasps her hand and says, "I know you will never cheat."

"No. I will end my relationship before I cheat." After dinner, Brooklin goes home. She does not return to the hotel.

Brooklin is delighted on Monday to return to her office. Being in the suite was inconvenient. Her telephone rings and interrupts her thoughts. "Ms. Covington, it's Agent Dalton. I want to inform you that I spoke to the Chief of Police and was told that the only listening device found was on your office telephone. During my visit to Logan Courtyard, I didn't enter your office. Therefore, I don't believe this wiretapping incident is associated with our witness. It's my understanding that Detective Ryan is rendering a full investigation into this matter. Our office will continue to monitor and maintain a close watch on any developments."

Brooklin asks, "Is Detective Ryan aware of the FBI's presence at Logan Courtyard?"

"No, and I must reiterate that only you and Attorney Jones should have this information. Ms. Covington, we do not feel our witness is in any danger and a move at this time would not be wise. I will keep you informed."

Brooklin places her cell phone on her desk thinking, okay Agent Dalton, your witness may not be in any danger, but what about Logan Courtyard? She provided the FBI access because she felt obliged to assist them with this situation. She walked into the fire with her eyes wide open. Therefore, now she has to just settle down and see it through.

Erica walks in and Brooklin's day begins. Around 1pm, Erica informs her that Detective Ryan is here. "Hi, Brooklin," he says, "have you eaten?" Her thoughts return to the conversation with Jill on Saturday.

"Brooklin!" Detective Ryan says.

"Oh, no I haven't eaten lunch. Actually, I only had tea this morning. I can call the restaurant and have them bring us lunch."

"Why don't we go out and grab some lunch. Then we can talk more freely."

Brooklin is a bit puzzled. "You don't think another listening device is in my office?"

"No I just thought you could let the computer work wait and we can have a quick lunch outside of the walls of Logan Courtyard. Breathe some fresh air."

"Detective, why don't we have lunch on my balcony? It's private and we can talk out there." He agrees, so they call and order lunch and move to the table on the balcony. It's a beautiful sunny day.

"You have a fantastic view of the courtyard from your balcony," he says. "There is always something to take pleasure in here at Logan from a stroll along the beach, the style and beauty of the hotel, the stunning scenery. It's an incredible experience."

"Thank you. I appreciate your accolades."

"Well, we thank you for such a grand hotel in our area. I talked to your security this morning regarding routine checks on your office and the surrounding area. Per your request, I questioned Max again to learn why he was telling staff members that there had been a hit on Larry. Max didn't have any information of his own but was repeating rumors he had heard from Jerry. I've decided to check the surveillance tapes and camera daily. I have also begun examining previous surveillance tapes dating as far back as two months."

"Thank you, Detective."

"You're not going to call me Greg, are you? You're going to continue referring to me as 'detective.'"

Brooklin smiles at him and says, "You have a problem with me calling you detective?"

"No, I rather like it," he says. Brooklin changes the subject and they laugh and talk about local news topics until their lunch arrives. Jerry places their lunch in front of them, then stumbles and almost falls as he leaves.

Brooklin watches Jerry carefully. "I'm

disturbed about Jerry's habits," Brooklin says after Jerry leaves the balcony. "I think I'll try to have a meaningful talk with him. He's a good employee, but I don't want an addict working at Logan Courtyard. I had similar problems with my brother, although my brother wasn't a good employee."

Returning for the lunch trays, Jerry brings coffee for Detective Ryan and tea for Brooklin. After he leaves, Detective Ryan says, "I questioned Lorna's friend John last night. He confirmed what Lorna told me. They both lack any factual information and are just repeating the rumors they have heard. Last night, I also talked to the two maids that were terminated, Mary and Joan. Neither had information relating to the case. And I questioned Taylor again this morning at her apartment. She is an angry, bitter woman. Even so, I didn't learn any new information regarding Larry's case. Nor do I think she or the terminated maids bugged your office."

"Were you able to question Larry at Memorial?"

Detective Ryan shakes his head and says, "Brooklin, this is a weird case. Mr. Carter is better today. He's able to open his eyes and speak. Therefore, I was permitted to question him." Brooklin concentrates on every word as he continues. "The victim was able to speak but seems somewhat reluctant to cooperate with me or investigators."

"He didn't say anything?" Brooklin asks.

"The victim would not talk. After questions were asked, he just looked at us."

"He wouldn't answer your questions? Are you certain he can speak or that he understood the questions?" she asks.

"Yes, both his doctor and brother told us Mr. Carter's speech is slurred and slow, but he can speak. He just would not talk to us. I'm uncertain if he's protecting someone or if he's terrified to talk," Detective Ryan says.

"Well, what now?"

"I keep searching for answers, go where the facts lead me and re-question individuals if necessary."

Brooklin smiles and says, "I guess that's what the public call police harassment."

He grins and says, "We do what we have to do to solve the case."

Then, he looks at Brooklin mischievously but before he can say anything more, Brooklin stands and says, "Okay, Detective, I have to return to work."

He laughs, "All right, I don't want to overstay my welcome."

Brooklin calls Colin and relays the information about Larry. Colin asks if she would come home early tonight and she tells him yes, she'll be home at 6pm. Then Brooklin calls Luke and gives him the same information. Luke and Brooklin talk for a few minutes. "Luke, I didn't have an opportunity to talk to you alone at dinner yesterday. How are you doing?"

"Mom, I'm doing okay."

"Are you sure?" she asks.

"I'm sure. I'll be glad when this situation is clarified with Larry. But other than that, I'm good. Mom, don't worry about me. I'm focusing on school and work. And Laila and I have been chilling." Brooklin tells him she loves him and returns to her work on the computer.

Luke goes into the kitchen to get a bottle of water when his telephone rings again. He runs to his telephone thinking, what did mom forget? "Hello."

"Luke, its Taylor." Luke is shocked.

He hasn't seen or heard from Taylor since that night in her apartment when she demanded her key. Luke had even deleted her phone number from his cell. Luke is silent. "Luke, are you there?"

"I'm here."

"How are you?" Taylor asks.

"I'm fine; however, I'm certain you didn't call me regarding my health."

"Luke, I wanted to ask if you could meet me at the coffee shop around the corner from my apartment tomorrow morning. Maybe before your 10am class?"

"Why, Taylor?"

"Well, I wanted to talk to you about something. Luke, can we meet?"

"What do you want to talk about, Taylor?"

"Well, the detective that is investigating Larry's case came to see me this morning. I really would like to talk to you about it," she says.

Luke thinks for a moment. "Okay, I'll meet you there at 9 tomorrow morning," Luke says.

"Okay, I'll see you then."

Luke puts the phone down thinking, "I

certainly did my best to distract myself and to date other girls. Yet here I am after a brief conversation with Taylor, feeling like the bottom dropped out of my stomach and realizing that I'm still deeply in love with her." He walks to his bedroom wondering what that call was really about. Does Taylor know that Larry said his name in the hospital? Feeling confused and frustrated, Luke shouts, "Will this ever end?"

Chapter 13

The next morning Brooklin arrives at work and finds that her office door is partly ajar. She hesitates and then pushes the door open. "Oh, Andy, it's you. I wasn't sure who was in my office. I guess, I'm getting a little paranoid."

"Paranoid? Why, Ms. Brooklin? Is it because of what happened to Larry?"

Brooklin realizes Andy doesn't know about the listening device on her phone. She says, "I'm sure that's probably what it is. How are you, Andy?"

"I'm fine, Ms. Brooklin. I heard you fired Ms. Taylor."

"Yes, Taylor is no longer employed here." After a few seconds, Brooklin asks Andy what he thought of Taylor.

"Oh, she was an unpleasant one."

"Really? No one told me."

"Yeah, she was not a nice lady. You know she was having an affair with your son, Luke?"

Brooklin looks at him stunned and says, "What?"

"Yes," Andy continues, "She's the type

that will chase a young man until she finally catches him."

"Do you know how long they were having an affair?" Brooklin asks.

"Well, I'm not sure. You didn't know?"

"I learned about the affair just before she was terminated. Andy, does anyone else know?"

"I think just Larry and me. We walked in her office and found them … um, shall I say, in a compromising situation? I think if anyone else knew, it would have quickly traveled through the hotel rumor mill. Larry and I, we'd *never* say anything."

"You say, Larry knew?"

"Yes, we walked into Taylor's office together and there they were. I couldn't understand why the door wasn't locked. Wouldn't that be the first thing you'd do in that circumstance?" said Andy, appearing a little embarrassed.

"Thanks for telling me, Andy. And please do not reveal this information to anyone."

"Oh no, Ms. Brooklin. I'd never tell anyone. Let me be on my way. You have a good day, Ms. Brooklin."

Brooklin begins to wonder if *that* was what Larry wanted to tell her that morning before the meeting. Is that what he was trying to tell her at the hospital? Maybe he wasn't saying that Luke was driving the car that hit him. Perhaps he was telling her that Luke and Taylor were having an affair.

Brooklin telephones Colin and tells him about her conversation with Andy. "Brooklin, do you really think this is what Larry was trying to tell you?"

"I really think it is. However, tomorrow I'll visit Larry. Colin, I really didn't think Luke was capable of committing such an offense. Speaking of Luke, I need to call him. I'll talk to you later." Brooklin phones Luke but there is no answer. She looks at her watch and sees that it's 9:05am. She realizes he's probably on his way to class. She'll call him later this afternoon.

Brooklin takes her morning walk around the hotel. Everything seems in order. Finally, the employees are becoming a united group. They are feeling more comfortable, speaking openly with one another and in their staff meetings. She begins to plan. Brooklin believes that by the end of the month, she can begin interviewing for a replacement for Taylor. She will continue to attend the regular weekly department head meetings. And she will have the private monthly meetings with each department supervisor and attend staff meetings bi-weekly. She thinks she's on the path to having a relatively unified staff and, therefore, ready to share some of her responsibilities with a capable assistant. She'll talk to Colin tonight. After she trains her assistant, she can spend less time at Logan Courtyard. As Brooklin turns the corner, she and Ron almost collide in the hall. He's talking on his cell phone and not concentrating on where he's walking. Hotel guidelines clearly state that staff members can use their cell phones only in their personal offices, the staff lounge or the private employee sections of the hotel. Ron looks at Brooklin and realizes he's probably in trouble. "Oh, Ms. Brooklin, are you okay? I'm sorry. I was talking to my mother."

"Ron, I'm certain you are aware that there are designated areas for employees to use their cell phones in the hotel, and the hallway is not one of them."

"I know, Ms. Brooklin. I'm sorry.

There's just so much happening right now. I assure you I will not talk on the phone again in the hallway and will follow hotel rules. "

"Ron, I would like to talk to you for a few minutes in my office. Let Tom know."

Ron looks at Brooklin and says, "Right away, Ms. Brooklin."

Brooklin returns to her office and Ron knocks on the office door ten minutes later. "Come in, Ron." He comes in, sits down, and looks everywhere except at Brooklin. "Ron, how do you like working at the hotel?"

"I like it."

"Everyone is nice to you?"

"Yes, everyone is friendly."

"And, how are you doing otherwise?"

He looks at Brooklin for a minute and then looks down and says, "Okay, I guess."

This kid is extremely shy, Brooklin thinks. "Ron, when having a discussion with someone, you really should look at them." He looks up at Brooklin for a few seconds and then looks down again. "I heard your father was improving."

"Yes, he's getting better."

"Ron, is there a problem at home? Is that why you were talking to your mother in the hallway?"

"Well, we are having some financial problems." He looks up at Brooklin and asks, "Ms. Brooklin, do you need more help here at the hotel? I could really use more hours."

Brooklin realizes Ron had looked at her the entire minute when he asked for more hours. She thinks, now that is progress. "Well, Tom told me you were doing a good job in the grounds department and that you have not missed a day of work. So, talk to Kevin in the restaurant. I know he needs some kitchen help."

"Okay, thank you so much, Ms. Brooklin."

"Well, don't thank me yet, Kevin hasn't hired you." Ron smiles and walks to the door. "Ron, I don't want you talking on your cell phone in any place other than designated areas."

"Oh, you don't have to worry about that, Ms. Brooklin."

As Ron walks out, she hears him greet someone and say that he's doing better. There's another knock on the door and it's Detective Ryan.

"Brooklin," Detective Ryan's says as he

enters her office with a smile and sits down. His demeanor changes a bit as he asks, "How is Larry's kid doing?"

"I think as good as can be expected. He's a hard worker. Larry is improving so I think Ron will be fine."

"Have you given any more thought to who may have planted the bug in your office?"

"Yes, but I really don't know. I don't have a clue."

"Well, I just returned from the precinct. We were discussing Larry's case. Larry's clothing has been analyzed. We were hoping to get some paint chips or something that would lead us to the car."

"Anything?" Brooklin asks.

"Nothing from his clothing. I have a computer printout of the cars in the area that fit the description of the vehicle that hit Larry. The problem is we checked each and came up with nothing."

"I understand it is a blue Mazda?" Brooklin asks.

"The crime scene was photographed to give us secure documentation of all the evidence including skid marks and tire impressions. Our experts analyzed them concentrating on where the point of impact took place. They noticed the change in the tire mark direction just before the impact. The rear wheels turned opposite the front wheels. There are presently only several vehicles in which this can occur. Therefore, from this information obtained from our experts and the details given by the witness, we believe the car that hit Larry was a blue Mazda 626." he says.

"Detective, I saw a blue Mazda 626 in our staff parking lot about two months ago. Our staff members are issued parking permits for their vehicles. I asked Erica to check employees' records; however, none of our employees listed a blue Mazda as their vehicle."

"Can you search for the parking permit information on your computer now?" Brooklin turns to her computer, enters the staff files and prints the parking permit documentation. He takes the paperwork and says, "Hopefully this information will provide some answers."

Around 6pm, Brooklin begins to make a list of individuals who have entered her office in the last few months and those who have a key card. Detective Ryan asks her to put pen to paper in an effort to help her recollection. She continues to wonder who could have planted that bug as she walks to her car. Brooklin unlocks her car and looks around the parking lot. She has a weird, eerie feeling that someone is watching her. She looks around the parking lot a second time but does not see anyone and she thinks, "Brooklin, you're probably just being paranoid again."

Chapter 14

The next morning, Larry is asleep as Brooklin enters his room. There are fewer tubes and his coloring looks better. Mark is not in Larry's room or in the hallway. Brooklin is hopeful that she will have a few minutes alone with Larry. Slowly, she walks to Larry's bed and says, "Good morning, Larry. It's Brooklin from Logan Courtyard."

Larry moves, turning toward her. He opens his eyes, blinks a few times appearing to become acclimated to the bright sunlight entering the room. "Brooklin?" he says in a low tone.

"Yes," Brooklin says. "How are you, Larry?" He smiles. "Larry, we're all so happy that you're improving."

He smiles again and says, "Thanks. Thanks for the flowers and fruit basket." He talks very slowly.

"You are welcome. Are you in any pain?"

"Yes, but I feel much better."

"Mark has been here every day with you."

"Yes, I know," he says.

"Where is Mark now?" Brooklin asks.

"He's at home taking care of a few things."

"Is it uncomfortable talking?"

"No," Larry says.

"I was here last week. Do you remember?"

"No, I don't remember."

"Larry, I want to talk to you a few minutes about my last visit. If at any time, you are uncomfortable or in pain, please let me know. I don't want to upset or distress you in anyway." He nods and looks at her questioningly. "During my last visit, you mentioned my son Luke's name. Do you know why you would have said his name?"

Larry says, "No, I don't recall."

"Larry, the day of your accident, you and I were standing at my office door. You told me you had something important to tell me. Do you remember what you wanted to tell me?" Brooklin looks at him intensely. The room is noticeably quiet and Larry looks as if he is thinking about the question. "Larry," Brooklin says, "are you okay? I don't want you to overexert yourself."

Then he says, "I wanted to tell you

188

about Luke and Taylor. The affair."

Brooklin takes a deep breath. "Okay, thank you Larry. I *did* learn about the affair. Was there anything else you wanted to tell me?"

"No, I can't remember anything."

"You did well, Larry. Thanks again. Are you feeling all right now?"

"Yes, I'm fine."

"Larry, do you remember what happened to you?"

He turns his head and says, "No."

"Larry, do you remember anything about the accident?"

"No, nothing." Larry turns, looks at her and murmurs, "Brooklin, be careful."

"Larry, what do you mean be careful? Be careful of what or whom? Are you thinking of the accident?"

He begins to get agitated, then says again, "Just be careful." Larry's breathing becomes rapid.

Brooklin says, "Okay, it's all right. I'll be careful." Brooklin makes an effort to put Larry at ease and change the subject. "Larry, I have to leave for work now. Would you like for me to turn on the television?"

"No, music" he says looking at the stand beside his hospital bed. Larry listens to a song from his iPod and Brooklin breathes a sigh of relief as she leaves his room. Brooklin can't wait to give Colin and Luke the good news.

Luke places his backpack on the chair in his bedroom. He thinks of his meeting with Taylor yesterday. She walked in with her low cut blouse and body-hugging jeans. She looked as beautiful, full of energy and sexy as he remembered. He told himself, "Remain focused."

Taylor ordered coffee and walked over to the table. "Luke, I hope I didn't keep you waiting."

"No, I just arrived. What did you want to discuss regarding the detective?"

"Luke, first I would like to know, how are you? What have you been up to?"

"Taylor, I'm fine and have to go to class."

"Luke, I want to apologize for the way I acted the last time we were together. Your mother had just fired me and I was very upset."

"I accept your apology."

"Luke, why are you so cold toward me?"

"Taylor, why am I here?"

"I would like to give us another try. Will you give us another chance?"

"Taylor, I have moved on. Is there anything more you would like to tell me?"

"Luke, come back to my place. Let's talk privately."

"Taylor, you really didn't want to talk to me about the detective, did you?"

"No, I just wanted to see you," she says.

Luke stands, "I have to go. I'm going to be late for class. Taylor, you take care." Luke recalled how quickly he walked out the coffee shop. He knew he was still obsessed with her and needed to leave before succumbing to that woman. It took every ounce of his willpower to walk away from her and the most fulfilling relationship he had ever experienced in his life. Although after he left the coffee shop, he continued to question Taylor's true motives.

Brooklin calls Colin from the car.

"Yes, Brooklin," Colin answers sharply. Brooklin questions, "What has happened to Colin and me? It's really sad." She looks in the rear view mirror and wonders if that is the same black Dodge she noticed following her out of the hospital parking lot.

"Brooklin?" Colin says sounding irritable.

"I'm here, Colin. I wanted to tell you that I talked to Larry. He confirmed he was trying to tell me about Luke and Taylor's affair. He also told me that he doesn't remember anything about the accident."

"That's good news, Brooklin. Have you told Luke?"

"No, I'll call him in a few minutes." Brooklin pauses for a moment. "Colin, are you willing to meet me halfway and work on our marriage?"

"Brooklin, I don't want to discuss this on the telephone."

"Colin, lately I've been coming home around 7pm and you've been arriving home after I'm in bed. I'm trying here, Colin."

"Brooklin, I'm at the Teen Center now and I don't want to delay a scheduled meeting."

"Okay, Colin, we'll talk later."
Brooklin thinks to herself, "I was going to tell him about Larry telling me to be careful. But he was in such a rush to get off the telephone."

Brooklin calls Luke. "Hi," Brooklin says, "I have good news. I just left Larry at Memorial. Last week when Larry said your name, he was trying to tell me of your affair with Taylor. He also told me that he doesn't remember the accident."

"Oh wow, that is good news and such a relief."

"I know, honey."

"Mom, I met with Taylor yesterday. She told me that she wanted us to get back together." There is complete silence. "I told her, I had moved on."

"Oh Luke, good!"

Brooklin thinks to herself, "Looking back, it seemed to me that Taylor became resentful of my inheriting the hotel. If she wanted more for herself then, she should have believed in herself enough to start her own business. I would have supported her. Instead, she resented and begrudged me because of my inheritance and chose to bite

the hand that fed her. And this is the
aftermath."

Returning to her call to Luke, Brooklin
asks, "I wonder what Taylor really wanted."

"Mom, that's exactly what I was
thinking. But, don't worry. I am absolutely
done with Taylor."

"That's good to hear. I'm at the hotel
now, so I'll talk to you later. Have a good
day."

"You too, Mom."

As Brooklin is getting out of her car,
she notices the black Dodge turning around in
the parking lot and leaving Logan Courtyard.
She thinks back to Larry cautioning her to be
careful and her earlier feeling in the parking
lot of being watched. She recalls how that
man in the hospital hallway knew her name.
He was enormous, really muscular and she
remembers the stoned look in his eyes. Who
was he? Brooklin also thinks about her office
being bugged and now she's wondering if that
black car was following her. She's not certain
if she is someone's target, but she will take
Larry's advice and be careful.

Brooklin glances at the clock in her
office, realizes it's after 1PM and orders lunch

from the restaurant. About ten minutes later, Jerry knocks and enters with her lunch. Wanting to talk with him, she asks him to place her lunch on the table and sit down for a few minutes. They talk for about fifteen minutes and come to an understanding. He tells her his drug habits were only recreational. Brooklin explains the only reason he is still employed at Logan Courtyard is because he is a good employee. She advises him that the hotel is implementing random drug testing and that a positive test will be grounds for immediate dismissal.

After lunch, Brooklin works until 4:30pm and tells Erica that she's leaving for the day. She has a hair appointment. She's giving herself the green light to remove Larry and the flurry of questions and suspicions from her thoughts for the remainder of the day. After the hair salon, she returns to Logan Courtyard and gets a full spa treatment, a relaxing way to get one's bearings. She feels amazing following her spa visit and arrives home feeling incredible and totally relaxed.

Of course, Colin is not home. Brooklin goes upstairs and puts on a casual dress. She thinks about going downstairs and getting a plate of assorted fruit and maybe some chocolates as well when she notices that Colin's closet door is open. She walks over to close it and notices that about half of his clothes aren't in his closet. Confused, she checks his bureau and realizes Colin must have moved out of the house. Brooklin utters, "Could this be true? He moved out without talking to me?" In a zombie-like state, she walks downstairs and sees the note on the kitchen table. She reads it, crumbles it and throws it on the floor. Colin feels they need some time apart. This will give them an opportunity to reflect, he writes--it will help them. He didn't tell her because he didn't want her to try to talk him out of moving. He'll be staying at the apartment at the Teen Center, he says. She looks at the note on the floor, "I can't believe this. Does Colin really think a separation is going to help us? Or is that the excuse he's using?" Colin will be home on Sunday for the family dinner, the note says, and they can tell Laila and Luke together. "How did I fail to see the signs? To recognize how bad things were between us?" Brooklin picks up the note from the floor and places it in the garbage can where it belongs. She curls up in the chair, finally releasing all the built up hurt and pain as the tears incessantly flow down her face.

Chapter 15

The next morning Brooklin explains to Maggie that Colin is now staying at the apartment at the Teen Center and that they will inform Laila and Luke on Sunday. Maggie looks sad and asks if Brooklin is okay. "I'm fine," Brooklin says. "I had my private pity party last night. And today, I return to work."

Brooklin arrives at the hotel around 7:30am anticipating the arrival of the contractors who will begin converting the last available space in the hotel into a small movie theater. The theater, limited to hotel guests only, will have an access door with the capability of opening onto a newly designed courtyard. The multiple outdoor screens with digital projection technology and crystal clear sound will make outdoor viewing the ultimate experience. This addition will allow Logan Courtyard the option of movies or live performances in the courtyard as well as the theater simultaneously.

Around 8am, the contractors arrive. Brooklin answers their questions and returns to her office before attending two department staff meetings. Her telephone beeps, it's an appointment reminder. She returns to her office and calls Laila. "Good morning, Mom," Laila says. Before Brooklin can continue, Laila interrupts. "I know you're calling to remind me of my yearly physical appointment with Dr. Levine this afternoon.

"Yes, honey, I am. How are you?"

"I'm fine, Mom. How are you?"

"I'm a little excited. Today is renovation day."

Laila laughs, "That's right, the movie theater and the new outdoor patio."

"Yes, courtyard."

"Mom, that is going to be so cool."

"I think so too. All right, I'm going to let you get ready for your appointment. Call me after."

"Okay, Mom, I'll talk to you later."

Erica comes in Brooklin's office and says, "A Mr. Griffin called. He's with Griffin Development and wants to schedule a meeting."

"I've heard of the company; however, I'm unsure why he would like to meet with me. Did you ask him why he wanted this meeting?"

"Yes, he said he has a business proposition he'd like to discuss with you. Since you're booked through Monday, I scheduled him for Tuesday at 4PM."

"Ok, Tuesday I guess I'll learn about this business proposition."

"Brooklin, are you going to allow staff members to have a movie night after the theater is completed? You know to 'break-in' the theater?"

"That's a thought. When I meet with Karen, we'll come up with a plan."

"Brooklin, Logan Courtyard will bring movies and the excitement of live and taped performances to life in its theater and courtyard. I am super excited."

"And we have to continually maintain our first-rate service in every area. I will give staff salary increases as their duties multiply with the new additions. I do not want the hotel's superior quality performance to suffer. Hopefully, the theater and new courtyard will pay for itself eventually."

"Brooklin, the cost of the popcorn and snacks in the theater alone should cover the cost of the theater. That is some mark-up." Brooklin shakes her head and they both laugh.

"Erica, you have no idea what this addition is costing me. However, you have to invest in your business and I'm hoping it will be the best money I ever spent. Therefore, I'm embracing this new addition and I'm not complaining."

Detective Ryan knocks on the door around 9:30pm. "When are you going to hire an assistant? You work too hard," he says.

"I could say the same about you. I'm surprised you're still here."

"I just returned from downtown. I haven't been able to locate Big Mel or his goon friends. I think they've gone underground."

"You think this Mel was involved in the hit and run?"

"He has a perfect motive. Larry owed him money. Still, I don't know if he's guilty or if I can eliminate him as a suspect. Right now, I'm just following the evidence. I also questioned Larry again today."

"Really? I visited Larry yesterday. He told me that he doesn't remember the accident," Brooklin says.

"Yes, well he did talk to me today. He told me that he didn't remember anything about the accident as well. However, I don't believe him."

"My visit was a little strange," Brooklin says. "Larry told me to be careful. When I questioned him about why, he became agitated, so I didn't continue. However, I'm beginning to consider his words of warning."

"We're still looking into who planted the bug in your office. Nonetheless, I think Larry knows more than what he's saying."

Brooklin decides not to tell Detective Ryan about her suspicion that someone may be following her. "How are you going to get him to talk?" she asks.

"I'm on it," he says.

"What does that mean?"

"I have a plan to get some results from Larry."

"Okay, I'll leave the police work to you."

"Brooklin, I'm going to the shooting range tomorrow. Why don't you come with me?"

"I don't think so, Detective. I don't like guns."

"Have you ever shot a gun?"

"No and I'm not interested in shooting

one."

"Brooklin, think about it. I'll be with you and can demonstrate the proper way to handle and fire a weapon."

"No, Detective. I told you, I don't like guns."

"Okay, I guess I'll have to remain really close and keep you safe from harm."

Brooklin ignores him and says, "Detective, here is the list of individuals I remember entering my office in the last couple of months. I hope I didn't forget anyone."

"We'll do another sweep on Friday. I don't think we will find anything, but we'll continue to randomly conduct sweeps."

"Sounds wonderful to me," Brooklin says.

"Can I walk you to your car?" he asks. "It's getting late."

"My car is in front of the building. I'll be fine."

"Brooklin, can I ask you a personal question?"

"It depends on the question."

"Are you happy in your marriage?"

"Detective, I'm not going to discuss my

marriage with you."

"Okay, you're right. I apologize. Are you ready to go home for the night?"

Brooklin thinks to herself, "No, I do not want to go to that empty house."

"Brooklin?"

"Yes, let me clean off my desk and I'll be ready." Detective Ryan walks her to her car. Brooklin drives home thinking that she might just move into one of the hotel suites upstairs. She's sure Lorna will tell Jamie and Linda that Colin is now staying at the Teen Center. Soon, her entire staff will know she and Colin are separated. During her drive home, she checks her rear view mirror a couple of times and determines that she is not being followed.

Brooklin works all day Thursday and arrives home around 11pm. Before leaving home Friday morning, she packs a bag. Brooklin talks to Detective Ryan briefly and learns that no other listening device was found in the hotel during the sweep. Brooklin thanks him and the officers and then talks to the contractors about progress on the theater. She works until around 10pm Friday night, walks around the corner to the elevator, presses 2nd floor, enters Suite 207 and locks the door behind her. She looks at the view of the tree-lined streets through the oversized picture windows. Brooklin thinks of the harmonious mix this area offers -- the beaches, the harbor, festivals, sensational shopping, cultural attractions and great food. She turns from the window and looks at the elegant surroundings of this one bedroom suite. She enters the bedroom, slips out of her clothes and grabs the luxurious bathrobe. She arranges the candles she brought from her office. In about ten minutes, Brooklin is soaking in the tub, candles lit with soft music playing in the background. She thinks of how wonderful the addition of the theater will be for the hotel.

Saturday, Brooklin works at the Teen Center until about 7pm. Colin, of course, isn't there. She returns home Saturday evening, takes a shower, gets in bed with her computer and finishes some work. Brooklin finally gets tired and falls asleep.

Brooklin prepares Sunday dinner for the family dressed in shorts and a t-shirt. She feels a little odd without Colin. They are normally in the kitchen together on weekends. After dinner is ready and the table is set, Brooklin sits on the couch with a glass of ice tea wondering how the kids will react to the news. They are older now, so she's hoping this separation will not have such an adverse effect on them.

Colin arrives first. He walks into the family room and sits across from her on the chaise. Their eyes meet. "Brooklin," he says and nods at her as if he's speaking to a distant acquaintance. What did Colin think? That she would argue with him and have a temper tantrum? No, she refuses to give him the satisfaction of knowing how this separation has hurt her.

"Hi, Colin, do you want anything from the bar or a glass of ice tea?"

"I think I will have a glass of your ice tea." He walks in the kitchen. Brooklin realizes the television is off and quickly reaches for the remote to conceal the awkward silence. Minutes later, she hears the voices and laughter of Laila and Luke. They are all smiles and full of silliness. She absolutely loves her children and looks forward to their company each and every

Sunday. She really hates to have this conversation with them. Soon, the smiles will disappear.

After the four of them finish dinner, Brooklin serves dessert. Colin waits until everyone is eating cake before he approaches the dreaded subject. "Guys, your mother and I need to talk to you about something important." Colin looks at Brooklin and then at Laila and Luke. They turn and look at their mother and then, Colin. There is silence, stillness. "First I would like to say, your mother and I love you very much. Nothing is more important than the two of you. However, your mother and I are going through a difficult time and I have moved into the apartment at the Teen Center. This, of course, has nothing to do with the two of you. And even though the physical status of the family unit has changed, we will still remain a family."

Brooklin looks at the shock on their kids' faces and says, "Although the two of you are older now and you're making your own decisions, your father and I will continue to offer our support in whatever way we can. I know this new restructuring of our family will be a process for all of us. However, I want you to remember that you can always rely on us."

Luke asks, "Is this because of what happened with Larry and what happened with Taylor and me?"

"No," Brooklin says. "This is only about the relationship between your father and me. Our separation is not in any way related to the two of you."

"The two of you didn't begin to have problems until you found out what was going on between Taylor and me," insists Luke.

"That's not true, Luke. We were having problems prior to your relationship with Taylor. The two of you just were not aware." Brooklin looks over at Colin for assistance.

"Listen guys, we realize that this announcement is a shock and there are feelings of hurt, sadness and maybe even guilt. But this is no one's fault. It just happened."

"Well, it's someone's fault," says Luke. "Dad, why did you move out?"

"Son, I thought it would give your mother and me time to sort through some things."

"What things?" Luke pauses and then continues. "And Dad, you couldn't do that at home?"

Laila speaks calmly, "I'm sure this is a difficult time for Mom and Dad, Luke. They didn't say they were divorcing. So, let's encourage them to work through their problems. No one wants our family to split up. So, Mom and Dad, have you thought about counseling?"

"No, we have not talked about counseling," Brooklin says. "The separation is new to us. However, counseling may be helpful. Right now, your father and I are trying to sort through these 'things' in our own way and at our own pace. We ask that the two of you be patient and allow us time to work through this situation." Brooklin really wanted to say "to move forward with our life," but she is aware they have to approach this subject with care for the kids.

Brooklin cleans the kitchen and the family room thinking about their earlier conversations with the kids. She realizes it is normal for the kids to be upset and a little angry. She and Colin have to continually show them love and support. They all agreed that they will continue with the Sunday family dinners. As Brooklin gets ready to return to Logan Courtyard after dinner, the telephone rings. "Hello, Mom," says Luke. "I'm going to move back into the house. I don't want you to stay in that big house by yourself."

"Honey, I appreciate your offer. But I probably will spend the majority of the nights at the hotel. Luke, I do not want you or your sister to think you have to take care of me. I promise you, I will be fine. I'm really concerned about the two of you. Luke, if you want to talk about the separation more, we can."

"No, Mom. I don't want to talk about it anymore. I really don't know what I'm feeling."

"You probably need some time to process everything. Your father and I want you and Laila to be okay and to know that we are always only a phone call away."

"Mom, no one will stay in the house? Our house will be empty? It will no longer be home or feel like our home."

"Honey, we will still have our Sunday dinners here. I will spend some nights at home. And Maggie is here three days a week.

Just remember, your father and I are here for you if you need us."

"Mom, I love you."

"I love you too, Luke. Listen, I don't want you to worry about your father and me. Just focus on yourself and your studies. I will talk to you tomorrow." Brooklin goes upstairs and packs enough clothes for a few days. Brooklin actually overpacks -- enough for a week. She decides to call Maggie before leaving for the hotel. Brooklin gives her instructions regarding caring for the house and tells Maggie that she will check on the house a few times during the week. Brooklin puts her phone in her bag, walks through each room, and pauses at the kitchen door. She looks back into the house, turns the lights off and sets the alarm. She closes the door and thinks, my home, our house.

Chapter 16

Monday morning, Brooklin is listening to the television in the suite while dressing for work when she realizes she forgot to pack underwear. How could she forget something like her underwear? Brooklin thinks for a minute, "You can just get a few pairs from the boutique downstairs. No, that might be a little awkward. I can envision the questioning gaze of the clerks now. 'Why is Brooklin buying panties?' Forget it, today I'll go bare." Brooklin finishes dressing and walks to the door telling herself it's no big deal. There are a lot of women who go panty-less.

At the weekly department head meeting, Brooklin asks Keith, the head contractor, to provide a brief presentation regarding the addition of the theater. Everyone is excited about the project.

Afterwards, Brooklin works in her office until around 12:15pm. Detective Ryan knocks on the door and enters her office. "Brooklin, it's a beautiful day. I suspect you wouldn't know this because you work in this hotel from sun up to sun down. You need to start enjoying life more. Live for the moment."

Brooklin thinks to herself, "I am, I have no undies on and it's giving me an incredible high and sense of freedom. I feel liberated and sexy just from going bare bottom. Who would have thought such a simple action could make a woman feel empowered? Can't underestimate the power of being pantiless!" Brooklin smiles to herself and realizes that Detective Ryan is still talking.

"Let the work wait. Go outside, take a walk and feel the sunshine on your face."

"Detective, I'm sure you didn't come to my office to try to liberate me. Have you found new evidence?"

"No, we carefully cross-referenced the list you provided of Logan Courtyard's employees and also individuals in their household vehicle registrations and we didn't find a match with the hit and run car. I checked the staff parking lot surveillance cameras and realized the hotel didn't place cameras in the staff parking lot until after Larry's accident."

"Well, we have surveillance cameras on the entire outside peripheral; however, we did not begin videotaping the staff parking lot until after this occurred with Larry."

"Well, if one of the staff members actually parked a blue Mazda 626 in the hotel's parking lot, surveillance footage would have led us to that individual."

"Detective I'm going to ask you again, do you think the person who hit Larry is an employee of the hotel?"

"I just follow the clues and the evidence."

"Well, are the clues and the evidence leading you to Logan Courtyard? May I have your opinion on this, Detective?"

"I try to remain impartial and approach the evidence with an open mind to see where it leads me."

"Well, what trail are we following today?" Brooklin asks.

"Today, I'm going downtown. I have a tip on where I may be able to find Big Mel."

"Well I guess I don't have to tell you to be careful," Brooklin says.

Detective Ryan flashes a big smile and says, "Oh, you are concerned about me?"

Brooklin looks at him and says, "Detective, just be careful. I am concerned about all of my friends." He laughs and walks out of her office thinking about his return to the precinct for an unmarked vehicle, "I hope a Dodge Charger is on the lot."

Brooklin is in the office working around 6:00pm and looks up to see Jill standing at the door. "Hi, Brooklin, I heard you never leave this place."

"Hi. What are you doing here?"

"I came to see you, of course."

"You heard that Colin and I are separated?"

"Yes, Colin told Levy. Are you okay?"

"Yeah, I'm all right. My thoughts are really focused on the kids. It's still early; however, they seem to be handling the separation reasonably well. If they are okay, then I'm okay. I'm actually having dinner with Laila and Luke on Thursday."

"Well, I'm glad you and the kids are supporting each other. Levy told Colin he should have remained at home and worked through the problems. He explained to Colin that separations can be dangerous."

"Well, Colin made the decision without talking to me. I really didn't think our problems were substantial enough for him to move out of the house."

"Brooklin, the two of you never discussed a separation?"

"No, I came home one evening and Colin was gone. And you know what's disturbing -- I spoke to Colin earlier in the day and he didn't mention he was moving."

"I know you are angry and you have a right to be."

"I'm not angry. I'm just tired."

"Brooklin, anger is a reasonable response. Why aren't you angry with Colin?"

"Well, apparently, Colin was not happy in the marriage. I gave my all to Colin and my family. I respected my marriage and asked Colin for approximately two years to develop Logan Courtyard. Colin and I both agreed to this commitment."

"Well, he told us that you worked late about four nights a week and he wanted you home."

"Jill, nothing or no one stopped Colin from visiting or working at the hotel. I may have worked some long hours; however, believe me when I say I took care of my man. Even with Laila and Luke living away from home, I provided for them as much as they would allow. I did not neglect Colin or my family."

"Well, I am angry at Colin for you. I just don't think Colin is being fair to you."

"I think Colin became jealous of my work at the hotel. He may have been home alone some evenings, but so was I for about fifteen years. Where is the emotional support for me? "

"Do you think he is having an affair?"

"I don't think so. But, I really don't know."

"Brooklin, you sound like you don't care."

"I'm just frustrated. I love my husband. But to answer your question, if I learn Colin slept with another woman before we separated, our marriage is surely over."

"What if Colin begins dating?"

"We are separated. And, who knows how long the separation will last or if it will eventually lead to a divorce. I'm not naïve enough to think Colin will not look at or date another woman."

"Are you saying this to give yourself permission to date?"

"No, I'm not. I'm not interested in entering into another headache. I just want to focus on work."

"Are you willing to forgive Colin and allow him to return?"

"Jill, I can honestly say, I don't know. We were married for over twenty years and he left without even having a discussion with me. At this point, I have lost faith in him."

"Brooklin, do you know how fabulous you are? You are a good person. Colin certainly made a mistake and I hope he doesn't take too long to come to that conclusion."

Brooklin looks a little distressed and says, "Okay, friend, let's change the topic."

"I just want you to know, I love you and I'm here for you." Jill turns and points to the bag on her arm. Brooklin looks confused. "You have a suite upstairs for me? Levy is out of town. I'm spending the night at Logan Courtyard. We are going to have a girl's nite." She points to her bag again and says, "I brought my pajamas."

"Jill, I'm fine. Go home."

"Too late, I brought my pjs. It's time you start accepting a little support. Let's go to Talb, have dinner and then go upstairs and watch movies." Brooklin stands still for a moment, hesitating. "Brooklin, let's go. I'm hungry." Brooklin cleans her desk, grabs her purse and gets ready for a girl's nite.

After leaving Brooklin and securing a vehicle from the precinct, Detective Ryan drives down Geer Boulevard slowly. People are on corners, in front of stores and just hanging out on both sides of the street. He parks near Grill 55, an eating spot and dance club. Detective Ryan gets out of the Dodge Charger and is approached by a woman wearing a long blonde wig, a halter top and shorts. "Hi, baby, you're new around here. Who are you looking for? You're looking for me?" Detective Ryan ignores the woman and enters Grill 55 with his badge in hand. He walks in to the sounds of music and people partying. A large bar is on the right; every bar stool is occupied and people are laughing and talking standing in pairs and in groups. There are three doors to the left of the bar. One leads to the kitchen and the two other doors he suspects are bathrooms marked M and F. Toward the back is a shabby dance floor and on the left are tables with worn chairs. Sitting at the first table is the one and only, Big Mel, talking on a cell phone. A second table is occupied with a muscular man who looks to be about 6'6 with broad shoulders and who is probably with Big Mel. Detective Ryan walks toward Big Mel. Big Mel looks at Detective Ryan and the strapping man stands abruptly, hand reaching in the back of his pants. Detective Ryan flashes his badge, and the man takes a step back but keeps his hand positioned on his weapon. Detective Ryan stands in front of Big Mel as he completes his phone call. "Okay, Jack, I'll call you after I take care of that for you." Big Mel puts the phone on the table and says, "Well, if it isn't Detective Ryan," he says with a grin. "Detective, what can I do for you? Can I buy you a drink?"

"Mel Jones, I have some questions regarding a hit and run on Bauknight Ferry."

"A hit and run?"

"Larry Carter was hit" and before Detective Ryan could finish, Mel says, "Yeah I heard about that on the news. But, Detective, why question me?" Big Mel looks to his left, nods and his sidekick removes his hand from his weapon and sits down.

"Mr. Jones, it is my understanding that

Mr. Carter owed you money."

"Detective, where are you getting your information from?"

"I'm asking the questions here, Mr. Jones. Did Mr. Carter owe you money?"

"Settle down, Detective," Big Mel says with a smirk. "That was true; however, Mr. Carter settled his debt."

"Mr. Carter paid you the money he owed you?"

"Well, I didn't say that. But I'm not in the habit of discussing my business deals."

"Mr. Jones, when was the last time you saw Mr. Carter?"

"I think about three months ago."

"And where and why did the two of you meet?"

"We met on the corner of 5th. It was time for Larry to settle his debt."

"And how did he settle his debt if he didn't pay you?"

"Now, Detective, that's between Larry and me."

"A few months ago," Detective Ryan says, "That would have been in January? When was this payoff?"

"Actually, I think it was the end of

January. It was like a birthday gift for an associate."

"And what associate would that be?"

Big Mel shifts in his chair and says, "Are we done here, Detective? I was about to leave for an appointment when you arrived."

"No, Mr. Jones, I'm not done. You were about to tell me which of your associates has a birthday in January."

"Detective, do I need to call my lawyer?"

"Mr. Jones, you can answer my questions here or at the precinct. I only have a few more questions, so what will it be? If you answer now, we both can make our next appointments."

"What other questions, Detective?" Big Mel asks as he repositions himself in the chair.

"Mr. Jones, a witness has placed you at Logan Courtyard a few months prior. Now that would be around the end of January."

"Detective, they must be mistaken. That Ms. Covington would not allow me or my friends in Logan Courtyard. She would have her security escort us out of the hotel and off the grounds."

"Well, a witness has placed you in Logan Courtyard's parking lot. Did you meet with Mr. Carter in the parking lot?"

Big Mel stops and thinks for a moment. "I don't know who would tell you that. Oh, was it that girl, the girl?" Detective Ryan doesn't answer. "What was her name?" Big Mel asks.

His sidekick shouts, "Taylor. Taylor is her name."

Big Mel looks at his goon friend like he would like to punch him in his mouth. He was trying to possibly learn from Detective Ryan who was revealing his whereabouts. Detective Ryan in return is amused at Big Mel's sidekick offering Taylor's name.

Big Mel insists, "No, no. Now that I think about it, I was told to make certain I didn't meet Larry at the hotel. I was never at that hotel."

"You were told by whom? Could it have been your associate whose birthday is in January?" the detective asks.

Big Mel, realizing he has said too much, shifts uncomfortably in his chair once again and says, "I mean, Larry told me he didn't want to meet at his job. Detective, I am

223

done talking unless you're going to arrest me. However, I will be out within the hour and I can tell you, I do have an alibi," he says smiling.

Detective Ryan looks at the men with disgust determining, "These two goons are as stupid as they look. They have just given me quite a bit of information. No wonder their boss wanted them to go underground. Now, I just need to locate this Jack that Big Mel was talking to on his cell. Could this Jack's birthday possibly be in January?"

Chapter 17

The next morning, Brooklin wakes around 7am, showers and gets dressed. Around 8am, Jill is at the door. "Let's grab breakfast and some coffee." At the restaurant, Jill orders an egg, cheese and turkey bacon croissant, yogurt and fruit. She loves to eat. Brooklin gets a cup of tea, a banana and half of a grilled bran muffin. Finishing her breakfast, Jill says, "Okay, I have to get to work. But first, I think I left my work bag in your office." They walk to Brooklin's office and find Jill's shoulder bag on the couch.

"Jill, I appreciate your support. Thank you for the girl's nite."

Jill smiles and says, "No problem." There is a knock on the door and Detective Ryan walks in. Brooklin introduces Jill to Detective Ryan. Walking to the door, Jill says, "It was nice meeting you, Detective Ryan."

"Likewise," Detective Ryan says as he turns his back to Jill and sits in the chair near Brooklin's desk. Jill smiles and mouths, "Wow, he's a hunk" and closes the door.

"Good morning, Detective. How are

you?"

"Good, Brooklin. Early breakfast with your girlfriend?"

"Yes," Brooklin says. "So, were you able to talk to Big Mel?"

"Yes" and he tells her about his questioning of Big Mel leaving out the part regarding Brooklin, Logan Courtyard and Taylor.

"How do you think Larry settled with Big Mel?"

"I went to the hospital to talk to Larry this morning. However, Larry apparently had a seizure and doctors are not allowing any visitors until he's stable."

"You're not going to answer my question regarding how Larry settled with Big Mel are you?" Detective looks at her. "Right, I remember. You just follow the evidence. Well, I'll phone Mark to check on Larry's condition and will let you know what I learn."

"Brooklin, has Big Mel ever been a guest here at Logan Courtyard?"

"Well, I can only say that I have no knowledge of Big Mel being a guest here. Why do you ask?"

"Just inquiring," he answers. "Would

you have a problem with someone like Big Mel staying at Logan Courtyard?"

"I do not have a problem with anyone staying at Logan Courtyard unless they carry out criminal acts. However, I do not want any unsavory presence at Logan Courtyard." Brooklin thinks briefly about their eleventh floor guests who have been very quiet and discreet.

"I have another question for you." Brooklin looks at him inquisitively. "Brooklin, I was wondering if you will have dinner with me tonight?"

She gazes at him, a little surprised. "Detective, I'm married."

"Brooklin, really? Where is your husband? He's never around. I would just like an opportunity for us to get to know each other outside of work. Let's be serious here. Are you really happy in your marriage?"

"Detective, please."

"Brooklin, you are sidestepping my question. I heard the two of you are separated."

She looks at him a little astonished. "Detective, I need to return to work."

"Brooklin, if this is the way he treats

you, he doesn't deserve you."

"Detective, you know nothing about the way my husband treats me."

"He left you and I can't imagine anything you could do that would make him want to leave you."

"My husband is a good man," Brooklin says assertively. "We just ran into a roadblock."

"Brooklin, I'm not trying to upset you."

"Then, don't," she emphasizes.

He stands and looks at her intensely. "I apologize if you feel my behavior is inappropriate." He walks out the door.

A few minutes later, Erica enters Brooklin's office, "Hi, are you all right? You're looking a little frazzled," she says.

"I'm fine. Just hoping this doesn't turn into an unpleasant day. Did you call Jill yesterday?"

"Yes, I thought you could use a friend. Are you upset with me?"

"No, but please don't do that again."

"Well, did you have a good visit with Jill?"

"I did. I always enjoy talking to Jill. Now, new subject. Apparently, you and the entire hotel know Colin and I are separated."

"Yes, I heard about it yesterday. I am really sorry. You loved Colin and were devoted to him, and this is how he treats you? He doesn't deserve you."

"Okay, tell me what you've heard?"

"The word is that Colin moved out of the house and into the apartment at the Teen Center. Rumor has it that you spend more time at the hotel than at home. Brooklin, do you think he's intimidated by your success at the hotel? Sometimes, men are threatened by successful women."

"Well, it is what it is. I'm really tired of discussing my marriage. However, I thank you for your support and concern."

Erica grins and says, "You will always have that. You are more than a boss to me. I think of you as a friend. Anyway, I'm going to have to take a couple days off from work. Do you think you can manage without me in the office on Friday and Monday?"

Brooklin smiles and says, "I will try. Is everything okay?"

"Yes, I received a call from my mother. She's returning home from vacation. She visited her two sisters in Florida for a few weeks and then, the three sisters went on a cruise for a month. She'll be returning home in a couple of weeks. So, I will travel to my mom's on Friday and begin to get her house in order for her homecoming."

"That is very nice of you. I'm sure your mother will be grateful."

"Brooklin, you know what I'm thinking. You have to get back in the game. He left you. You shouldn't park yourself here in the hotel day and night. Take charge of your life. Have some fun."

Brooklin smiles and says, "Why thank you, Erica. I appreciate the advice." And they both laugh.

Given Brooklin's many conversations regarding her marriage, she gets a late start on her work day. She works in her office until about 5:00pm without pausing for lunch. Erica has left for the day and Brooklin's hungry. Earlier she snacked on a bag of fruit and nuts. However, now she's really wants some food. She smiles to herself and thinks, "Jill, what have you done to me? I do not even want my usual salad. I guess I'll take a walk to the restaurant. It will give me an opportunity to clear my head." There is a knock on her door and she thinks, "What now? I need some nourishment."

Detective Ryan enters with two large bags. "Brooklin, peace offering. I brought you dinner. You have to eat."

Brooklin smiles and says, "I have to eat. Detective, if this is going to turn into a discussion about my marriage…"

He interrupts, "It will not. We are just going to eat and be cordial."

Brooklin smiles and asks, "What's in the bags?"

The detective brought an enormous amount of Chinese food. "I wasn't sure what you liked so, I actually bought almost everything on the menu."

Brooklin laughs and says, "It looks like it." Then he pulls out a bottle of wine and two wine glasses. "Perfect" she says and he looks at her with a warm smile. They sit on the leather couch, eating, watching primetime programs, laughing and talking.

After the late news, Detective Ryan stands and says, "Brooklin, I had a good time. Thank you."

"Thank you" she says. "I haven't eaten Chinese in a long time. The food was enjoyable, it was good to unwind and the company was nice too." They look at each other and then Brooklin looks away.

"Brooklin, can we end the evening by taking a short walk along the beach?"

Brooklin thinks for a moment and says, "Sure." Outside, the temperature has dipped to about 68 degrees. The night is aglow with moonlight glimmering across the water and stars dancing across the sky. It's a spectacular, magical night as they stroll along the sandy beach listening to the gentle rush of the waves. They continue in silence as they return and begin to climb the stairs. As they reach the balcony and the door leading to Brooklin's office, the Detective moves before her, takes the keys from her hand and opens the door to her office. He walks in, looks around examining her office and after about thirty minutes of walking along the beach with shoes in hand, they finally speak. He looks at her and gently says, "Good night, Brooklin, I had a wonderful evening."

"Good night, Brooklin says."

After Detective Ryan leaves, Brooklin sits on the couch enjoying the ambiance, not wanting to move. A few minutes pass and

Brooklin begins to tidy up after a perfectly delightful evening. Later in Suite 207, she takes a long shower, puts on her nightgown and climbs into bed. However, she can't sleep. She's wide awake and decides to phone Jill. "Jill, did I wake you?"

"No, Levy doesn't return until tomorrow and I don't sleep well when he's isn't home. I'm in bed watching late night. What's up?"

Brooklin tells Jill about her evening. "It was truly wonderful. The best evening I've had in a long time. Jill, I really like him. Even though Colin and I are separated, I'm struggling with being attracted to this man because I still feel married. But, Jill, I haven't felt like myself in a long time and being with him makes me feel like me again."

"Well, Brooklin, is that a bad thing?"

"Jill, I'm separated and the detective is really charming. I'm afraid if I begin to see him outside of work, it will be cheating. And what if I begin to really care for him? What about my children, my family?"

"Brooklin, that is the very reason why Levy told Colin that separation can be dangerous. You know, I want you and Colin to resolve your issues. However, Brooklin, you were a good wife to him. He left you. You don't owe Colin anything. If you want to see Detective Ryan outside of work, it will not be cheating. Honey, you are separated."

"Okay, I have to really think about this. I have to take my time. My family is important to me. Thanks, Jill."

"Honey, you are welcome. Remember, you did not create this situation. Colin did. And consider, you would not be entertaining the thought of seeing Detective Ryan if you were still with Colin."

"That's true."

"Furthermore, you need to let go of the past. This is not the same as what happened with Lydia. You have to live this life as best you can. Stop with the guilt. If you decide to see Detective Ryan, you will not be doing anything wrong."

"Thanks again, Jill. Good night." Brooklin grabs one of the large pillows from the bed and holds it close to her thinking, "Jill always makes me feel better."

Chapter 18

Taylor opens her door and sees Detective Ryan standing there. "Good morning, Ms. Daniels. I need to ask you a few more questions regarding Mr. Carter's hit and run. May I come in for a few minutes?"

"Detective Ryan, I have answered all your questions. I really don't have anything more to add to what I've already told you."

The detective walks past her and into the apartment before she has a chance to invite him in and says, "Well, maybe after hearing my questions, you may recall some information you neglected to tell me previously."

"Well, please come in and have a seat," she says sarcastically.

"Ms. Daniels, when I questioned you previously, you told me you did not see Mr. Carter the day of the hit and run. Is that correct?"

"Yes, that is correct."

"Ms. Daniels, you were seen by a witness with Mr. Carter the afternoon of the hit and run."

"Well, we work together. Therefore,

there is a chance that I did see him on that day. I don't recall."

"Ms. Daniels, you told me previously you *definitely* did not see Mr. Carter the day of the accident. Which is it? Did or didn't you see Mr. Carter?"

"Well, I guess I forgot. If someone saw me with Larry then I must have seen him that day."

"Ms. Daniels, were you having an affair with Mr. Carter?"

"No, I was not."

"I was told that Mr. Carter was looking for you at the hotel the afternoon of the hit and run. Ms. Daniels, why was Mr. Carter looking for you that afternoon? What did the two of you discuss that day?"

"I don't know. It probably had something to do with work."

"Ms. Daniels, I'm giving you an opportunity to explain. I would advise you to take advantage of it." She doesn't answer. "Can you tell me again, why you were fired from Logan Courtyard?" She gives the detective a dull stare. "You're still not answering." He hesitates a moment, then continues, "You want to hear what Ms.

Covington told me?"

"Okay, I was fired because I was sleeping with the Queen Bee's son."

"And, it had nothing to do with Mr. Carter?"

"Detective Ryan, why don't you tell me. You have all the theories."

"I don't work with theories, only the facts. Now, let me ask you again. Your firing had nothing to do with Mr. Carter?" She begins to perspire. "Ms. Daniels, you appear to be sweating. You look like you're about to explode."

"Detective Ryan, what do you want?"

"The only agenda I have is to hear the truth."

"Larry knew I was having an affair with Luke. He told me that he would tell Brooklin about the affair if I didn't sleep with him. However, I made him a different offer."

"What was the offer?" asks the detective.

"I offered to give him money. I heard that Larry had a gambling problem. So, I offered him money."

"Is that why he was looking for you?"

"Yes, I agreed to pay him $1,000 that

day or he threatened to tell Brooklin. However, it didn't matter. He told Brooklin and I lost my job."

"I see. Mr. Carter was blackmailing you. I'm going to ask you again, where were you on the night in question?"

"Detective Ryan, I was not driving the car that hit Larry. I was with Luke Covington that entire evening."

"What time were you with Mr. Covington?"

"We were together from the time we left the hotel around 7pm until 7:30am the next morning."

"Did anyone see the two of you leaving the hotel?"

"No, we left about ten minutes apart and our cars were parked in different areas."

"Did anyone see you and Mr. Covington between 7pm and 7:30am? Can anyone verify Luke and your whereabouts during this time period?"

"No. We were alone and we made sure my neighbors didn't see us."

"Quite interesting. Ms. Daniels, I can imagine what kind of position you were placed in being blackmailed. It was a delicate situation, knowing that if Mr. Carter told Ms. Covington about you and Luke, you might be fired. Ms. Daniels, that gives you a motive."

"I'm not lying to you. I wasn't on Bauknight Ferry that night. Ask Luke."

"Well, Ms. Daniels, I definitely will be verifying your story. You've lied to me twice already."

"Well, please do. Now, are we done here?" she asks sullenly as she stands.

"One last question, Ms. Daniels. Did Mr. Carter ever mention Big Mel?"

She looks alarmed and quickly tries to hide it. "No, he didn't."

"Ms. Daniels, do you know Big Mel?"

"No, I do not. Detective Ryan, I have told you all I know and I am running late for an appointment."

"Okay, Ms. Daniels. If I have more questions, I know where to reach you. You're not planning to leave town, right?"

Taylor glares at him, "No, Detective Ryan, I'm not." The detective leaves wondering what Taylor's connection is with Big Mel and why didn't Brooklin tell him about Taylor and Luke's affair.

Detective Ryan walks down the

hallway at Memorial Hospital until coming to Larry's room. He knocks and, when no one answers, enters the room. Larry is asleep. The detective walks over to his bed and calls his name. Hearing no answer, he bends down, runs his hand behind and under the table next to the bed. Larry's brother Mark enters the room. "Detective, you shouldn't be in Larry's room. The doctors haven't given clearance for Larry to be questioned again."

"I'm sorry," says Detective Ryan. "No one was at the nurses' station so I walked down to the room. How is Larry doing?"

"Detective, you have to leave. Please call the nurses' station before visiting Larry. They will inform you when the doctors have given the approval for questioning."

"All right, I'm leaving. I hope Larry will improve soon."

The detective returns to the precinct. At his desk, he thinks about all the facts and interviews surrounding this case. "Where am I not connecting the dots?" he asks himself. He phones Brooklin. "Hi, how are you today?"

"I'm fine, Detective."

"I just returned from the hospital."

"Were you able to talk to Larry?"

"No, he still can't have visitors. Brooklin, I questioned Taylor again this morning and I asked her why she was fired from Logan Courtyard."

"What did she say? Did she say, I fired her because she was sleeping with Luke?"

"Yes."

"Well, that is partially true. I actually fired her because she was not performing her job duties and because of insubordination."

"Brooklin, why didn't you tell me that Taylor and Luke were having an affair?"

"Well, it's not something I wanted to broadcast."

"Brooklin, I didn't say broadcast. Why didn't you tell *me*?"

"I really didn't want to talk about it and I felt it was unrelated to the case. I viewed it as hotel business."

"Brooklin, is this an example of a mother protecting her child? Right now, I need to have knowledge of hotel business to solve this case."

"Well, my apologies for not providing you this information. However, Luke does not need protecting. Luke and Taylor's involvement is not related to Larry's case."

"Brooklin, I need you to be open and share all information with me. Allow me to decipher what is important."

"Okay, Detective, for you Logan Courtyard will be an open book." Brooklin thinks to herself, well *almost* an open book.

"Good. Hey, I really enjoyed last evening."

"I did too," she says. There's silence.

"My sergeant has asked me to help another detective for the next couple of days. Therefore, I will be here at the station and won't return to Logan Courtyard until Monday. You have my number. Call me if you need me."

"I will be fine, Detective." Brooklin puts the phone down, a little relieved. "Hopefully, this time away from the detective will remove him from my thoughts," Brooklin conceives. And since there is no time like the present, Brooklin focuses on work.

Thursday around 5pm, Erica and Brooklin walk to their cars. Laila and Luke have invited Julie and Brooklin to dinner at their apartment. Julie has moved out of Laila and Luke's place and into her new apartment. Laila answers the door. "Wow," says Brooklin, "who cleaned the apartment?"

Luke says, "Laila and I."

"Good job. It would have been nice if the two of you would have kept your bedrooms at home looking as nice as the apartment looks."

"Mom, have a seat at the table. We are going to serve you and Julie," says Luke. Laila sets plates, a box with a 24-cut pizza, an assortment of pastry treats, bottled drinks and water on the table.

"Placing a pizza box on the table is serving us?" says Brooklin. "I thought the two of you were cooking."

"Right," Luke says and everyone laughs.

Brooklin says, "I know my body is in shock. I had Chinese last night and tonight, I'm having pizza."

"Mom, you had Chinese food last night?" asks Luke.

"Well, someone at the hotel must have ordered food. We know you didn't place the order," says Laila laughing. Brooklin wonders if she has an unusual look on her

243

face. What prompted her to say that? She doesn't need to have that conversation with Laila and Luke. They continue to talk, Brooklin joins in and the four eat pizza.

Brooklin decides to work at the Teen Center on Friday instead of Saturday. The kids told her at dinner that Colin would be playing golf on Friday and would be at the Teen Center on Saturday. She would prefer not to talk to Colin until Sunday's family dinner. At this point, she didn't want to think about anything dealing with their situation. She leaves the hotel at 9:30am on Friday and asks Karen to call her if there are any problems. She arrives at the Teen Center a few minutes later. She and Laila drive into the Teen Center's parking lot at the same time. Laila gets out of her car, "Hi, Mom."

"Hi, Laila, I didn't realize you were here today."

"I had a couple exams this week so I took Wednesday off to prepare. Today is a make-up day. It works out well because it's field day and we need as many hands as possible." As they walk into the Teen Center, one of the volunteers stops Laila and begins a conversation. Brooklin continues down the hall to her office and works until about 12:45pm when she hears a "Hi, Brooklin." She sees her brother Jim standing in the office doorway.   She smiles, "Hi, Jim, how are you?"

"I'm good," he says as he sits in the chair in front of her desk. "How are you? Are you okay? I heard you and Colin are separated."

"I'm okay. What can I say, you have to handle what life throws at you."

"I couldn't have said that any better myself. However, I hope the two of you are able to work out your problems."

"Thanks, Jim. That's very nice of you to say."

"Do they have any suspects regarding Larry's hit and run?" Jim asks.

"No, they're still investigating. Did you know Larry well?"

"Not really, we just spoke when passing in the hallway. I tried to keep my distance from him."

"You did, why?"

"I was dealing with his ex-wife."

"You were seeing his ex-wife?"

exclaims Brooklin.

"Yeah, but I had to cut her loose. I was doing some things I shouldn't have been doing. But I stopped and I'm working on turning my life around."

"Jim, that's wonderful. I'm so proud of you."

"Thanks. Brooklin, I'm sorry for my behavior at Logan Courtyard. The things I was doing made me irritable, disrupted my relationships and interfered with work. I just was not thinking clearly or functioning well."

"Jim, that's over," Brooklin reassures him. "I'm glad you're doing well now."

"Yeah, I take it hour by hour and one day at a time."

"Well, you look good. Now, you said you were involved with Larry's wife?"

"Yeah, Carmen. Larry did a number on her. She drank more than I did. I tried to get her to stop drinking. But she wasn't ready, so I had to leave her alone."

"Her son, Ron," Brooklin says, "works at the hotel."

"Yeah, Carmen is not nice to that boy. And it's sad, he's a good kid. But she so centered on hating Larry."

A volunteer comes to the door and says, "Jim, we need you outside for the field day. All the kids are waiting."

Jim stands, looks at his sister and asks, "Brooklin, you going to join us?"

She thinks for a minute and says, "Yes, I think I will." Brooklin changes clothes and spends the remainder of the afternoon flying kites, running races and having a good time with family and the Teen Center's teenagers. During one of the races, she runs against Jim and Laila. They have so much fun, Jim does his usual bragging and, of course, Laila wins the race. Brooklin leaves the Teen Center about 6pm and returns home, soaks in the tub and falls asleep in bed watching television. About 10pm, she hears talking downstairs and finds Laila and Julie lying on the couch watching television. "What are you guys doing here?" Brooklin asks. "Laila, you didn't mention you were coming home tonight."

"Mom, Luke and I have decided to spend two nights a week at home," says Laila. "Luke is not here tonight because he has a headache."

"Guys, you don't have to do this,"

Brooklin says.

"Mom, just think of it this way. The food in the refrig will not spoil with big head Luke coming over two nights a week."

Julie laughs and says, "What about your square head?" Everyone laughs.

Laila and Julie decide to spend the night at the house, but Luke remains home in bed with a headache. He is about to fall asleep when the doorbell rings. Thinking it's probably one of Laila's buddies, he decides not to answer the door. His head is pounding. He changes positions to get comfortable but whoever is at the door repeatedly rings the bell. He gets out of bed thinking the person at this door will regret their persistence. He looks through the peep hole and sees that it's that detective. "Aww man!" Luke says as he opens the door.

Detective Ryan walks in. "Mr. Covington, you look awful."

"I have a headache and was in bed," Luke answers.

"I need to ask you a few more questions regarding Mr. Carter's hit and run," says Detective Ryan.

"Can this wait until tomorrow? My

head is pounding and I don't think I have the energy or am able to concentrate enough to answer your questions tonight."

"Mr. Covington, I only have a few questions. I'll make it quick."

Luke rubs his head and mumbles, "What questions?"

"When I questioned you previously, you told me on the night Larry Carter was hit by a car that you were with a friend."

"That's correct."

The detective continues, "I didn't pressure you at that time. You told me the friend you were with could confirm your whereabouts."

"That's right."

"Well now, I need to know the name of the friend you were with on that night."

Luke rubs his head and replies, "I was with Taylor Daniels."

"What time were you with Ms. Daniels?"

"We were together that night from 7pm until the next morning, around 7:30am."

"You were with Ms. Daniels all night?"

"Yes."

"Where were you and Ms. Daniels?"

"We were at her apartment."

"The two of you met at her apartment?"

"Well, we left the hotel and drove to her apartment in separate cars."

"Did anyone see the two of you leaving the hotel?"

"No, we always made certain no one saw us. And we parked our cars in different areas."

"Can anyone verify that you and Ms. Daniels were together from 7pm until 7:30am on the night of Mr. Carter's accident?"

"No, we made sure no one saw us together."

"Were you and Ms. Daniels having an affair?"

"Yes."

"How long were the two of you having an affair?"

Luke says, "I think about two months."

"Who knew about this affair?"

"I think just two of Logan Courtyards' employees."

"Which two employees?"

"Andy in maintenance and Larry in security."

"How did they learn of the affair?"

"They walked in Taylor's office and saw us together."

"And when did this happen?"

"I don't know. Maybe a couple of weeks before Larry's accident."

"Did anyone else know about this affair?"

"My mother learned about Taylor and me a few weeks ago."

"How did your mother learn of the affair?"

Luke thinks for a moment and then says, "She said Larry told her."

"Did your mother learn of the affair before or after Mr. Carter's accident?"

"After. She visited Larry in the hospital and he told her at that time."

"I would think that you and Ms. Daniels would be very upset about Mr. Carter discovering your secret relationship."

"No," says Luke. "It wasn't like that. I asked Andy and Larry not to tell anyone about Taylor and my relationship. Both said they wouldn't tell anyone. They said it wasn't their business."

"Did you tell them to keep quiet or did you give them a warning?"

"Detective, I asked them. And, before we go any further, let me just inform you that I had nothing to do with Larry's hit and run. I'm not that type of person."

"Well, it's a little convenient for you and Ms. Daniels to provide an alibi for each other. And you say no one else can confirm your and Ms. Daniel's whereabouts during those twelve hours?"

"That's right, no one else can."

"Did you say that you and Mr. Carter were friendly?"

"No, I wouldn't say we were friendly. I would say we were cordial."

"What about Ms. Daniels and Mr. Carter's relationship?"

"I think they were cordial as well. Taylor was Larry's supervisor."

"Was there any other connection between Ms. Daniels and Mr. Carter?"

"No, Detective Ryan. What are you asking?"

"I'm asking if there was some connection between Ms. Daniels and Mr. Carter."

"If you are asking if Taylor and Larry were involved, the answer is 'no.' "

"And you are certain?"

"I am certain. Larry is not Taylor's type."

"Explain what you mean by type."

"Larry gambles. Taylor is very meticulous about money. She doesn't even play the lottery. Taylor is really into saving money. She wouldn't be involved with Larry." Luke massages his head.

"We're almost finished, Mr. Covington."

"Detective Ryan, as you are aware, I have a really bad headache. I feel you are repeatedly asking me the same questions."

"I'm trying to get clarity, Mr. Covington. I only have a few more questions. Why do you think Larry told your mother about your affair with Taylor?"

"I do not know. I think that's a question for Larry."

"Mr. Covington, what have you heard about the hit and run? Have you heard any rumors regarding who was driving the car?"

"No, nothing. I have not heard who was driving the vehicle that hit Larry."

"Last question, do you know or have you heard of a man called Big Mel?"

"No, Detective, I do not know nor have I heard of a man called Big Mel."

"Okay, Mr. Covington, thank you for your time."

Luke closes the door behind Detective Ryan when suddenly he realizes he *had* heard of Big Mel. When he injured his ankle and was at the hospital with his mother, they overheard a lady in the next room mention how a Big Mel had attacked the patient because of money he owed. "Well," Luke thinks to himself, "if the detective would have waited until tomorrow when I was feeling better to question me, I would have been thinking more clearly and would have told him about what we heard at the hospital. But what about my statement regarding Taylor? Should I have told the truth? I wasn't with Taylor on the night of Larry's accident -- we were together the evening *before* the accident. Well, it's too late to change my statement now. I'll just have to remain Taylor's alibi." Luke turns, runs to the bathroom and vomits.

Brooklin works at the hotel a half day on Saturday and arrives at Maggie's house for dinner at 4:00pm. Since Colin left, she has more of a social life. She enjoys an afternoon at Maggie's and returns to her suite at the hotel around 8:30pm. She showers and gets in bed early. "Tomorrow morning," she says to herself, "I'll return to the house and prepare Sunday dinner.

Colin and Brooklin are amiable during dinner. It's a little strained at first. However, Laila and Luke engage them in conversation about what happened during the week and they are thrust into their normal, enjoyable Sunday routine. Luke comes into the kitchen as Brooklin is about to bring the dessert into the dining room and tells her about Detective Ryan's visit. As Brooklin listens to Luke, she is becoming increasingly annoyed, "It upsetting to me that Detective Ryan would subject you to such an interrogation, Luke."

"Mom, its fine. Although I wasn't feeling well, I conducted myself appropriately and answered all of Detective Ryan's questions." Luke leaves out the part about providing an alibi for Taylor.

"I'm sure you did, Luke. I will be happy when Larry's case is solved."

"I know, Mom, me too."

Later after dinner, Colin asks if he can

help clean the kitchen. Brooklin tells him
"no," that Luke has volunteered to help. After
Luke leaves to return to his apartment,
Brooklin drives back to her hotel suite.

Chapter 19

Mondays are always hectic and Brooklin finds herself moving from meeting to meeting and engaging in dialogue that normally she entrusted to Erica. Today is the last day of Erica's vacation. The two days without Erica revealed her importance to Logan Courtyard, especially with the vacancy of the Assistant General Manager's position. Brooklin realizes she has to hire more office help and replace Taylor soon. Erica arranged for a temporary secretary; however, Erica knows what Brooklin needs before Brooklin knows what she needs.

Brooklin finally returns to her office at 1:15pm with a salad and bottled water. She finishes her lunch and phones Jill. "Hi, it's Brooklin."

"Hi, how is it going?"

"Well, it's Monday and Mondays are always busy. That's one reason I am calling. I'm interested in hiring Karla. Colin decided not to hire Karla to work with Lorna, but now Logan Courtyard will need more office support with the new additions."

"You're in luck, my friend. Karla was

offered a job right after you interviewed her. However, she wasn't really interested in the position, besides she was out-of-town transporting the last of her furniture from her old apartment to her new townhouse here. I think Karla told you, she relocated back to this area to be near her family. She called last week informing me she is unpacked and ready to look for employment again. Therefore, I think this will work out well, Brooklin, being that she was really excited about the prospect of working for Logan Courtyard."

"Perfect," says Brooklin. "I'll have our team perform the background check and if all is satisfactory, we can discuss a starting date. Oh, sorry, Jill, someone is at my door. Talk to you soon, Jill, and thanks."

In walks Detective Ryan. "Brooklin, I see you have new help."

"Good morning, Detective. Erica is taking a couple vacation days." Brooklin is displeased with Detective Ryan considering his demeanor when questioning Luke. "Detective, Luke told me you questioned him Friday night."

"Yes," he replies, "I needed to ask him a few questions. His name had been mentioned when I questioned Taylor."

"Right, you have to go where the facts lead you," Brooklin says glaring at him.

"My questioning of Luke upsets you?"

"No, your behavior during the questioning upsets me."

"Brooklin, I have to be objective. I have a job to do."

"Well, if you would excuse me, I have a job to do as well. Good bye, Detective."

"Brooklin, come on now. Don't do this. We are both professionals."

"You knew he didn't feel well, why couldn't the questions wait until Saturday?"

"Brooklin, Luke is not a child. He's a young man. He handled my questions like a pro. He's smart like his mother."

"Don't try to charm me, Detective."

"Brooklin, I'm a detective working on a hit and run case. I was not hard on Luke. It was just clear-cut questioning. Will you give me a break?"

"Like the break you gave Luke?"

"Brooklin, are you serious?"

"Detective, today has been a demanding day. I need to get back to work," she says.

"Brooklin, don't be annoyed with me. When I met you, I wasn't looking for a special woman. Yet, I found her in you. And if there is any friction between us, I don't want it to be because you are annoyed with me." He reveals that wicked grin. "Seriously, Brooklin, relationships have always been hard for me. But there is this connection between you and me. Can't you feel it?" Brooklin doesn't answer and wonders how the conversation changed so quickly? "Brooklin, I look forward to seeing you every day." Brooklin opens her mouth to respond when the detective continues. "No, Brooklin let me finish. When I see you, I get this feeling. Is it just me? Are you feeling this … this spark?"

"Detective, I can't get involved with another man right now. I don't know where my relationship stands with my husband."

"You don't know where your relationship stands with your husband?" asks the detective. "You are separated. I just want to take you out occasionally and show you a good time. I'm not asking for a commitment." He smiles and says, "at least not right now."

"Greg," says Brooklin.

"You called me Greg. That's progress." Brooklin gives him a look. "Okay, it's baby steps. But, I will accept baby steps." He flashes that big grin as Brooklin shakes her head and they both laugh.

Colin suddenly appears at the door. He walks in and says, "Excuse me, Brooklin, do you have a minute?" The two men eye one another.

Brooklin is shocked at Colin's unexpected appearance in her office. "Detective Ryan, this is my husband, Colin. Colin, Detective Ryan." Neither man moves to shake hands. They just look at each other. "Detective, if you will excuse us please," Brooklin says.

"Okay," says the detective, "I have to go back to my office for a few minutes. When I return, we can resume our conversation."

Colin watches as Detective Ryan leaves the office and moves to close the door. Colin turns and asks, "Brooklin, can we sit on the couch and talk for a few minutes?"

"Sure" she says looking a little confused. Brooklin is wondering if there's a problem with Laila and Luke.

Colin sits closer than Brooklin would like. "I returned to the house last night to talk to you, but you weren't there." Colin says.

"I spent the night here at the hotel."

"Alone?" he asks.

"Yes, Colin, alone. What is it that you need to talk to me about?"

"I made a mistake, Brooklin. I should not have moved out of the house. I love and miss you so much. Brooklin, I'm sorry. I took you for granted. I had a woman who understood and appreciated me and who was not afraid to kick me in my butt when I needed it. I met my match in you and I think you met yours in me."

Brooklin is stunned! "Colin, do you think you can walk in and out of my life on an impulse?"

"Brooklin, you are a unique and remarkable woman and I made a mistake by letting you go. I want my wife back."

"Well, you should have thought about that before you walked out on our marriage without even the decency of discussing it with me." Brooklin moves on the couch so as to place additional space between them.

Colin hesitates a moment as he notices

her movement away from him. "Brooklin, let's be honest. I told you I missed you and how lonely the house felt without you."

"Colin, yes, let's be honest," says Brooklin quietly. "I gave everything to our marriage and family. You never had to worry about home. When you traveled or worked late, I welcomed you with open arms when you arrived at the door. Now when I ask you for time for Logan Courtyard, you move out of the house without talking to me. So I have to ask the question, how stable was our marriage?"

"You are absolutely right. I agreed to give you that time at Logan Courtyard, but I didn't realize how difficult it was going to be," says Colin. "You were working late and I was missing you. And it made me a little crazy."

"You don't think it was difficult for me all those years when you worked late and traveled? I was missing you too, plus I had the responsibility of our family. However, I stayed committed. Colin, many times I asked you to come to the hotel. You chose not to. Before I terminated Taylor's employment, if you asked me to come home early, I gladly came home. Colin, you needed to talk to me, to communicate with me. We could have worked on this together."

"I know and it's unfortunate. It took this separation for me to value the relationship we had. Brooklin, it's easy to put all the blame on me. But you didn't even call me after I left. It seemed like you didn't care. Why didn't you fight for us?"

"Maybe I would have fought for us if you had discussed a separation with me instead of just leaving. I definitely feel there is more you're not telling me."

"Brooklin, let's take a vacation. Let's go wherever you would like and spend some quality time together."

"Colin, running away will not solve our problems."

"It's not running away," he says. "It's an olive branch. We need time to work on our marriage."

"No, Colin. I'm going to finish what I started."

"Are you saying 'no' to a vacation with me or to my returning home?" Colin asks.

"I'm saying 'no' to both. I need time to think. I've loved taking care of you and the kids. I don't regret one minute of my time with my family."

"Well, Brooklin, it's sounding like you are resenting it."

"That's not what I'm saying, Colin. I'm telling you, I changed during our relationship. Relationships bring out different characteristics in people, which is fine. I became a nurturer like most women. And I loved nurturing you and the kids. Except, somewhere along the way I lost myself. I need to take the opportunity now to rediscover me."

"Brooklin, I didn't ask you to be something you didn't want to be. Now, I feel like you are blaming me for as you say, 'losing yourself'. If you didn't want to do it, why did you do it?"

"Colin, I nurtured my family because I wanted to ... my family is important to me. I wanted my children and our marriage to have a strong foundation. I'm just saying within the process, I relinquished me, the person inside. I'm not angry, it was my decision. However, Colin, you are not without some responsibility because you went along with it, you benefited from it."

"And that means you can't give us another chance?" asks Colin. "Think about the kids."

"I can't believe you. Did you think about the kids when you walked out? Colin, are you listening to me? Are you really hearing me?"

"I heard you say that you're not willing to give us a chance to repair our marriage."

Brooklin shakes her head. So many thoughts are racing through her mind … "Colin is refusing to really comprehend what I'm saying … I've tolerated this behavior too long and now he feels entitled … We married too young ... I'm like Lydia … I sacrificed myself and Colin took advantage. Now I want to change and Colin is not willing to allow me the transformation." Brooklin looks at Colin and realizes he is still talking.

"Why is that, Brooklin? Is it because of how I reacted with Luke regarding Larry's case? Because I didn't want to fire Lorna?"

"Colin, it's because you walked out on me, you didn't care about working through the rough times and because you didn't support me. And I will say this one more time, Colin, I did *not* ask you to fire Lorna.

I'm not going to lie and say I wouldn't have probably asked at a later time. However, you know I'm always willing to find a middle ground."

"Brooklin, I have not been with any other woman since I married you twenty-three years ago. What about you? Have you been with another man?"

"No, I have not."

"What about that detective? What is going on between the two of you? Is he the reason you're not allowing me to return home?"

"As I just said," answers Brooklin, "I have not been with any other man including Detective Ryan. Our problems are between us – between you and me. Don't bring anyone else into this situation."

"Brooklin, what will it take for you to let me come home? Can we stop looking back and look forward instead?"

"Colin, I think our relationship was tested and you dropped the ball. You left me and now I'm going to take the time to get in touch with myself – my needs, my desires … come into being again."

"Well, Brooklin, I think whether I left

or not, you were going to take the time for your needs and desires."

Brooklin stands abruptly, "Colin, I have to return to work now."

Going to the door, Colin turns and says, "Well, I'm not giving up on you or our family" and walks out the door.

Brooklin sits down thinking how her head is about to explode. "I need time to find some inner peace," she tells herself. "I have to focus on what makes me happy. Right now, it's my children and my work. I know I'm at a crossroad. And I plan to travel slowly to a new beginning. I do not need anyone's' permission or anyone to tell me in which direction to travel or at what speed."

Colin is leaving the hotel when he meets Detective Ryan. Colin stops and says, "Detective Ryan?"

"Yes," Detective Ryan answers.

"What are your intentions regarding my wife?"

"Being that you left your wife, I don't think I have to answer that or any other questions you may have."

"My wife and I are going to work out our problems. So, I'm asking you to not interfere."

"Oh, I'm sure you *want* to work out your problems with Brooklin. However, had I been fortunate enough to have a beautiful and captivating woman like Brooklin, I would have never let her go.   So, I have to thank you for providing me this opportunity because, otherwise I wouldn't have even gotten a second look."

Colin's voice rises as he says, "I'm not going there with you, Detective Ryan. Just don't interfere."

"You say, not to interfere." Detective Ryan smiles and says, "I'm looking forward to all the possibilities with Brooklin. I'm going to support her, appreciate her and do whatever I can to make her happy. I'm hoping she will open her heart and mind to a future with me."

"What? Do you actually think Brooklin will divorce me and marry you?"

"I hope so. If you had treated her better, we wouldn't be having this conversation. Brooklin is a wonderful woman and deserves to be treated as such."

"Detective," insists Colin, "I'm not going to debate this with you. Brooklin and I are married."

"Colin, you and Brooklin are separated and I'm putting you on notice. I'm interested in Brooklin and I'm not backing off."

Colin steps towards the detective and says in an elevated tone, "Well, I'm not going to hand over my wife to you."

"Then, game on Colin. Brooklin will have to make the decision. Now if you will excuse me."

Colin watches Detective Ryan walk into the hotel and probably straight into Brooklin's office. He gets into his car and hits the steering wheel. His mind is racing. "Everything Detective Ryan said was true," he thinks. "I have no one to blame but myself. What was I thinking to leave Brooklin? Now is it too late? I can't even imagine not being with Brooklin. I miss holding her in my arms. I've got to fix this. I'm going to pursue her like never before and, hopefully, she'll remember how good we were together. Maybe, we can rekindle what we had. And if that doesn't work, there are the kids. I will use the 'reuniting the family' card. I am going to pull out all the stops. I'm not going to let my wife walk out of my life.

No way is that happening. Detective Ryan, you will not have my wife, not my Brooklin."

Chapter 20

Tuesday morning Erica walks in Brooklin's office smiling. Brooklin greets her, "Erica, I'm so happy you have returned."

"Thanks, Brooklin," says Erica. "This package came for you."

Brooklin takes the package and opens it.

"What is it, Brooklin?"

"It's from Marion and Veronica. Their YumMe polish. Marion and Veronica are interested in having their YumMe products displayed and sold in our boutique."

"Well, Brooklin, what do you think?" asks Erica.

"I'll have to give it some thought. Now, how did everything go at your mother's?"

Erica explains, "It went well. I was a little anxious and worried, but I finally got everything accomplished."

"Good," says Brooklin, "I'm glad it went well. While you were gone, I realized how much work you do around here. I totally missed you. Therefore, I've decided to hire you some help."

"What? You're not going to lay me off? Are you?" asks Erica.

"No, of course not. You're irreplaceable. However, I know there's work you can allocate. You and I will brainstorm regarding duties for the new office worker. She will also assume some of Kathy's responsibilities as well. We'll talk about it later. Now, you walked in with a big smile. So, what's going on?"

"I've been thinking," says Erica. She looks at Brooklin with a sly grin. "Tomorrow, I'm going to Speed Dating. I'm available and ready to date again. Want to come with me?"

"What?" says Brooklin. "No, I would *never* go to Speed Dating. Now you mentioned, you are available *again*? I didn't know you were involved with someone."

"Well, it wasn't serious. It was just …" Erica hesitates, choosing her words carefully "a liaison with benefits. Anyway, I really don't want to talk about it. Brooklin, come with me to Speed Dating. You need to have some fun."

"No, I'm not interested in that type of fun."

"Well, you'll be missing a good time,"

Erica says.

"I'll count on you to tell me all about it."

"Brooklin," asks Erica, "This may be a wild question but what do you think about having Speed Dating here at the hotel? Maybe once or twice a year?"

"No, Erica. Now don't you have some work to do, being you have been out of the office for two days?"

"Okay, just a thought," Erica smiles as she leaves the office.

Shortly before 4pm, Erica buzzes Brooklin saying, "Mr. Griffin from Griffin Development is here."

"Thanks, Erica. Ask him to come in."

A tall man, who looks to be about 6'2, 300 lbs. and roughly 60 years old walks in and extends his hand. "Ms. Covington, it is a pleasure to meet you," he says in a low baritone voice. Brooklin motions for him to have a seat. "Ms. Covington, you have an exquisite hotel here."

"Thank you," Brooklin says. There is something about him that makes her feel a little cautious.

"Ms. Covington, I'm going to be direct

and come right to the point of my visit. I would like to buy Logan Courtyard." Brooklin looks at him showing no emotion. "Here is my offer." He writes a number on a piece of paper and passes the paper to Brooklin who looks at the offer and passes the paper back to him.

"Mr. Griffin," replies Brooklin, "I am not interested in selling my hotel."

He smiles. "Ms. Covington, I'm being very gracious. It's not guaranteed I will offer that amount next time. You know about business deals. Things can happen and things can change." He has a cynical grin on his face.

"Gracious or not, Mr. Griffin, my hotel is not for sale."

"Ms. Covington, what can I do to persuade you to sell Logan Courtyard?"

"There is not anything, Mr. Griffin. You have completely disregarded my rejection of your offer. Nevertheless, I assure you that no line of argument, incentive or astute plan would entice me to sell. Now, if you will excuse me. I appreciate your interest. However since I'm not selling Logan Courtyard, I think nothing else will be accomplished here."

"Ms. Covington, I don't want to upset you. You are such a beautiful woman. I don't like watching that nasty irritating wrinkle line appear on that gorgeous face. Can't we work this out?"

"Mr. Griffin, apparently you wanted my attention and you got it. However, my patience is wearing thin," replies Brooklin in a controlled voice.

"Ms. Covington, politics can be a dirty game."

"Mr. Griffin, are you threatening me?"

"Of course not, Ms. Covington. I don't go around threatening people. I'm simply stating, you don't want to lose everything you built here. I know you have invested a lot of money and time in this hotel."

"Who says I'm going to lose anything? Mr. Griffin, I think you underestimate me. However, you are not the first and probably will not be the last."

"Relax, Ms. Covington, I'm just making a statement."

"Even the most durable fabric wears out, Mr. Griffin. I really don't have time to sit here and listen to your attempts to coerce me into selling my hotel." She stands and says, "Good day, Mr. Griffin."

"You are smart as well as beautiful. However, there is an offer on the table. Why don't you take it, stay home and take care of your family or start yourself another business. Maybe, a clothing store."

"Now, you are trying to insult me. However, I'm not insulted or frightened by your type. You discredit yourself, Mr. Griffin, coming in my office and thinking because I'm a woman, you can intimidate me."

"It's not like that, Ms. Covington."

"All right, perhaps you are an equal opportunity offender." Brooklin looks at him intensely and continues, "After all the work and time I've dedicated and invested, you think I will just *give* my hotel to you?"

"Not give. We have given you a sizable offer for this hotel."

"Who are *we*? Who are you receiving your instructions from?"

Mr. Griffin looks at Brooklin angrily, "I don't take instructions from anyone."

"I'm sorry, Mr. Griffin, did I make you feel uncomfortable? A little uneasy? I'm noticing a nasty irritating wrinkle line appear on that fine-looking face."

He laughs. "Ms. Covington, I must say, I have enjoyed this exchange. However make no mistake, I intend to own this hotel."

"Who's your partner, Mr. Griffin?"

"I work alone, Ms. Covington."

"Okay, Mr. Griffin, if you are not going to answer my question then this meeting is over. This has been interesting. However, I'm a little tired of doing this dance with you. Therefore for the last time, Mr. Griffin, I completely reject your offer."

"Okay, Ms. Covington, I'll leave. But I hope you will give some thought to our conversation." As he stands, Brooklin notices his shirt has large wet rings under his arms.

"Great," she thinks to herself, "I got to him as well."

Brooklin thinks about the conversation with Mr. Griffin. She calls her lawyer, Levy, briefs him on her meeting with Mr. Griffin of Griffin Development and asks for a detailed report on this man. "Mr. Griffin has some skeletons in his closet," Brooklin says. "I want to know everything there is to know about him, his family, his associates and if there is a connection with any type of illegal activities. Research him relentlessly, Levy. I need an extensive report, including all the dirt. Even if you feel information isn't important, include it anyway. It may prove to be valuable.

"Levy, I'd also like you to contact TJ, Inc – they do our background checks. Please obtain their assistance when possible without giving them any particulars. Also have them to do a second background investigation on all our employees. Levy, inform them to use good judgment when gathering information. Griffin is a very shady character. I'd prefer that he not know I'm having him investigated. However, I'm not going to lose sleep if he learns of the investigation. He probably expects me to do some probing into his background. Levy, one final request, I do not want anyone to know about my conversation with Mr. Griffin including Colin."

Levy replies, "Okay, I hear you, Brooklin. We'll pursue your request thoroughly. And I will make certain we locate the dirt on Mr. Griffin."

After her conversation with Levy, Brooklin phones Colin. "Colin, I forgot to tell you when you were here. The hotel will be swept again tomorrow for listening devices. I intend to ask Detective Ryan about having our house swept for devices as well."

"Brooklin, I will take care of having a sweep done on our home. You do not have to ask Detective Ryan. Are you dating him?"

"No, we have eaten together a few times in my office, but I'm not dating anyone presently."

"Presently? Are you thinking about dating?"

"I'm not sure, Colin. I'm taking life as it comes one day at a time and I owe you no explanation about my personal life."

"Does that mean you don't mind if I begin dating?"

"Colin, you have to live your life. You didn't consult me before moving out of the house, so why do you need my input now? Colin, I have to go. Take care."

She ends the call and walks out on the balcony. Thinking, remembering, assessing, she says to herself, "Brooklin, you are not obligated to anyone. It's time you shift to survivor mode. You're smart and people will learn you are indeed a formidable opponent."

Chapter 21

Erica gives Karla a tour of Logan Courtyard on her first day of work. Brooklin welcomes Karla, tells her she's in good hands with Erica, and asks Karla to stop back at the end of the day for a brief meeting. Brooklin takes her morning walk around the hotel then attends two department meetings. She's in her office at 2:00pm when Detective Ryan arrives. As he enters the office, Brooklin thinks she probably will miss him when Larry's case is solved. She's beginning to look forward to their visits and enjoys their talks during the day. "Hi, Brooklin. How's your day going?"

"Good, Detective, what about yours?"

"I'm feeling pretty good today. The sweep results are good again. No listening devices were found."

"Oh that is good news," Brooklin says.

"I know you haven't eaten, so what about a business lunch?" She looks at him with apprehension. "Brooklin, a business lunch. Besides, I have somewhere to take you."

"Take me?" she asks with uncertainty.

"Take me where?"

"Brooklin, for once, throw caution to the wind and just say 'yes.' "

"Okay, then, yes!" she answers.

Detective Ryan leaves no time for her to change her mind. "Did you say, yes? Well let's leave now. I don't want you to have second thoughts." Brooklin informs Erica that she's leaving for a few hours and asks her to tell Karla that they'll meet in the morning.

While waiting in the hall, the detective phones a favorite restaurant for a special reservation for two. "Perfect," he thinks, "couldn't be better!" As the detective walks Brooklin to his car, he thinks how patiently he's waited for this opportunity. He didn't want to stand by and allow Colin to return to Brooklin's life. He's determined to do whatever he can to build a relationship with her. He knows exactly the perfect restaurant for their impromptu tryst -- an elegant and intimate Italian Steak House. When they arrive, they are escorted to a private candlelit dining room. A waiter pours their champagne and the detective notices that Brooklin is admiring the view of a perfectly cascading terrace leading down to a stunning flower-filled park. "Detective, this is magnificent. I love the restaurant and the grounds. It's beautiful."

"I made the reservation after you agreed to have lunch with me. Brooklin, can you call me Greg, at least during this lunch?"

"Greg, this is lovely. It would be easy to forget it's the middle of the day with the candles and the soft music."

"I just want you to relax and enjoy yourself. You deserve that."

"What happened to our *business* lunch?" asks Brooklin.

"Well, I'm sure part of our conversation will include business." Greg orders their lunch and the food is delicious – appetizers, soups, salads, marinated grilled chicken breast and dessert.

"Greg, is Larry's case any closer to being solved?" asks Brooklin.

Greg thinks to himself, "I have this beautiful date and all she wants to talk about is a criminal case." He smiles at Brooklin, "I think we're getting close to solving the case."

"Who do you think is the guilty party?"

"Brooklin?" Greg says raising an eyebrow at her.

"Okay, Greg, let's go in a different direction. I don't recall you telling me what happened with the questioning of Larry's ex-wife and Ron."

"Well, I questioned them right after the hit and run. We were not able to locate Mark, so we notified the next of kin. They were shocked to learn of the accident. They both were home and we accepted their alibi of being at their residence together during the time of the hit-and-run."

"What do you think of Carmen?" asks Brooklin.

"Well, I could tell she had been drinking, but she answered my questions well enough."

"What about Ron?"

"Ron also answered my questions satisfactorily. Why do you have so many questions about Larry's family?"

Brooklin answers, "I think Carmen has been mistreating Ron."

"What do you classify as mistreating?"

"I think Carmen has been verbally abusing Ron since she and Larry divorced, maybe even since Ron's childhood. What were your thoughts when you were questioning them?"

"Well," says Greg, "Ron was very quiet, only speaking when asked a question. Carmen was rude to Ron a few times while we were there. Thinking back, I think you might be right. However, Brooklin, I don't think you should get involved."

"I'm just concerned. He works at the hotel, you know, and he's very polite and a hard worker. I think I might just help him get his own apartment."

"Brooklin, you are assuming Ron wants to leave his home."

"Well, it doesn't hurt to ask."

Greg tells her, "I'm going to the hospital to question Larry later and I'll ask him his thoughts on this matter. Larry has improved and I have the doctors' permission to question him again."

Brooklin abruptly changes the conversations and asks, "Greg, do you have children?"

He looks a little stunned by the question and then says, "No, I don't. My ex-wife couldn't have children. So, I guess it wasn't meant for me to have kids."

They finish their lunch and champagne

and sit quietly for a few minutes with their own thoughts. "Brooklin, you ready for your surprise?"

"My surprise? I thought our having lunch was my surprise."

"No, I want you to brace yourself for the second part of our lunch outing. I think you will enjoy it."

"Well then, I'm ready for part two. Greg thanks for lunch. It was wonderful. The food was amazing."

They drive about five miles and arrive at a shooting range. "Greg, a shooting range? Look how I'm dressed. I'm wearing a pantsuit."

"Come on, Brooklin. They are having a ladies day. Now that you are separated, you may find yourself home alone and you need to know how to protect yourself."

"Well, I hope I never have to protect myself using a gun," Brooklin says as she places her suit jacket on the car seat. "Greg, let me just tell you, the thought of guns makes me nervous."

He smiles and says as they walk inside, "Well, you can always lean on me." Inside, the sounds are loud and the gun fires are like tiny explosions. Greg obtains their shooting kits and after they reach their assigned lane, they put on their ear muffs and goggles. Greg reaches in his jacket and removes a gun from its holster. Brooklin is speechless. She wonders, "Has he always carried a gun? I never really thought about Greg carrying a weapon. But, of course, he carries a gun – he's a detective."

"Brooklin," Greg explains, "we're going to practice today with my .45 automatic. Look at my stance. The hips should be at a 45-degree angle but the left leg should be forward and the right leg back. Okay, now, try the stance." Brooklin stands as he tells her. Greg looks at Brooklin's shoulder length black hair and sexy body. Her nice, large round breasts, the long alluring legs. That perfectly rounded firm butt and thinks, "Oh God, do I want this woman."

"Greg, am I standing correctly?"

"Yes, very good Brooklin." Greg demonstrates the hand grasp, front sight and the correct way of shooting a pistol, and then shoots the .45. Brooklin observes as Greg hits the target at center mass. "Okay, Brooklin, first we'll practice shooting the target with an empty gun." Greg stands behind Brooklin and positions the gun in her hand. It's heavier than she expected. He places his hand over her hand, his trigger finger over hers. Brooklin is very aware of the closeness of his body, and the warmth of his touch sends quivers through her. His finger slowly presses hers straight back against the trigger. After several repetitions, she is sensing several things including what a good shot feels like.

"Okay, Brooklin, time for you to shoot the target." She holds the .45 as Greg illustrated, aims at the paper target and slowly squeezes the trigger. The recoil startles her. "That was good, Brooklin. Now, try again." After a few shots, she calms down as she began to know what to expect.

After shooting several rounds, her anxieties are gone. Brooklin starts to feel a little comfortable and begins to show off saying, "Target, take that." Greg laughs and Brooklin realizes that she is somewhat enjoying this. As they leave the lane Brooklin says, "I still don't really like guns. But after today, I know I can fire a weapon and not shoot myself."

"Brooklin, did you enjoy yourself?"

"I did. I'm looking forward to returning and continuing target practice. Greg, when we arrived, I saw a number of self-defense devices at the counter. Can we take a closer look at their defense products?"

Brooklin decides to purchase a couple of items and as they are leaving, Greg says, "You should think about applying for a gun license."

"Greg, baby steps please."

He laughs and says, "Okay, baby steps."

As they drive away from the shooting range, Brooklin calls Erica. "Hi, how is everything?"

"Brooklin, everything's fine. Don't worry about the hotel. If there's a problem, I'll call you. Enjoy your afternoon."

"Thanks, Erica. I should be there within the hour," says Brooklin. She finally feels comfortable with her staff and the day-to-day operations of the hotel. Her thoughts return to that obnoxious Mr. Griffin. And, of course, after all my hard work, he would like me to sell! Never! It took a lot of work to get this far. Now, I'm supposed to take a back seat?"

Greg notices she's distracted and says, "Brooklin, it's been a long time since you have had an afternoon away from the hotel. Enjoy yourself."

Brooklin lays her head back on the seat and takes in the scent of Greg's cologne. She looks out the window and suddenly notices the building ahead --Griffin Development. She sits up abruptly. "Greg, what do you know about Griffin Development?"

Greg looks at the building and says, "It is a beautiful building, isn't it?" Well, Griffin Development is big business. Mr. Griffin's legal business includes buying commercial real estate. We think he has some illegal business ties as well, but we haven't been able to obtain enough evidence to prove it. I've heard the FBI is currently building a case against him. He's a sly one. Why do you ask?"

"I saw the building and just wondered about the owner," says Brooklin.

It's quiet for a few minutes then Greg says, "Brooklin," he hesitates a moment and says, "Brooklin, thank you." Greg reaches over and gives her hand a squeeze. The electrical energy in that touch doesn't escape either of them. They look at each other momentarily and Brooklin breaks the spell by moving her hand and asking, "Thanks for what?"

"What you just said helped me put together part of the puzzle. I can't believe I didn't realize it earlier."

"Realize what?" asks Brooklin. "What did I say?"

It's finally coming together!" Greg says.

"Well, I'm glad I could help," Brooklin comments as she sits back, continuing to think about what Greg said about Mr. Griffin. Brooklin wonders, "What Mr. Griffin and his partner want with her hotel. Is it for the legal or illegal side of the business?" Then, she realizes they are traveling in the opposite direction of the hotel and asks, "Where are we going?"

"We're here, on Bauknight Ferry. This is the crime scene," Greg remarks as he parks the car. They get out of the car and Greg looks down as if he's examining the road and the row of homes. He indicates which house is Larry's.

"What are we looking for?" Brooklin

asks.

"The impact took place here," says Greg.

Brooklin looks at the tire marks on the road and asks, "Larry was hit here?"

"Yes," answers Greg. I'm looking for anything we may have missed." Greg walks gazing in different directions. He stops, thinks and starts walking again. After about fifteen minutes Greg says, "All right, let's go."

Back in the car, Brooklin asks, "Greg, did you find what you were searching for?"

"I was trying to find something to use if Larry chooses not to answer my questions later."

"Did you find anything?"

"No, I'm just hoping my previous plan worked."

Brooklin returns to the hotel still glowing from her afternoon with Greg and finds Laila sitting on the couch in her office watching television. "Hi, Mom, where were you?" Laila presses the mute button on the television.

"I had some things I had to take care

of," says Brooklin. "So, what's going on with you?"

"Nothing, I was at home bored and I decided to come visit my mom."

"Well, I'm glad you did. Let me buzz Erica and tell her to hold my calls. So how are you and Luke doing?"

"Mom, we are okay. We just want you and Dad to resolve your problems."

"I know you do, but you and Luke need to focus on yourselves." Brooklin sits on the couch and continues, "Laila, I want to talk seriously with you for a few minutes. You know I only want the best for you and Luke. I'm not sure what the future holds for your father and me. We love each other, but I'm not sure that's enough. Laila, I never talked to you about my childhood. My parents worked hard and were good providers. But they were not affectionate people. I knew they loved me, but they never said those three words during my childhood and I didn't really feel the love.

There was always something missing in my life, like inside there was this small hollow area. Later as I matured, I looked for the person I was in a relationship with to supply enough love to fill the void that was within me. However, it never happened. Eventually, I realized no relationship or no one else can fill that void or make me complete. Only I can by loving myself. Therefore, I'm finally taking responsibility for my happiness and fulfillment. I am moving forward and trying *not* to let the cycle continue with my children. Otherwise, I'll be stuck in the same place trying to fill something that only I *alone* can fill and pass this behavior to my children."

Laila asks, "Is that why you are overly affectionate, with the hugs and saying 'I love you' all the time?"

Brooklin answers, "I'm sure that's part of it, but it's also because I love my family so much." She grabs Laila's face in her hands and kisses her on the forehead. "I was married to your father for twenty-three years. I love him and I enjoyed our life together. However, I think I gave so much of myself because I wanted to be needed. I was trying to fill the emptiness and somewhere along the way, I completely lost me. I don't want you to think I regret my life with your father. I do not. If I hadn't married your father, I wouldn't have my two wonderful children that I love and adore. I just wish I could have loved myself more. I'm currently making the effort to reclaim my life, trying to become whole. Now that you and Luke have left home, I'm trying to find value and meaning in my life again. Do you understand what I'm saying?"

"I do, Mom," Laila says as she hugs her mother. "I hope dad is patient, supports you and the two of you can come together again."

Brooklin smiles and says, "You are so smart." She looks up at the television news and suddenly notices Detective Ryan being interviewed on the steps of the precinct. She picks up the remote, presses the mute button and listens to the report. Laila turns to the television with curiosity.

"We are confident that the hit and run driver will be apprehended," says Detective Ryan. "We are committed to finding the driver. It's my number one priority."

"Do you have any leads?" asks Ms. Lark, the TV reporter.

"We do but, as you know, I can't share that information with you and compromise this investigation. However, I can tell you that we are grateful for the abundance of tips we have received. Our department checks every lead."

"No matter how outrageous?"

Detective Ryan smiles and says, "I didn't say that, Ms. Lark, you did."

Laila looks at her mother and says, "That detective is hot."

Brooklin ignores her and continues watching.

The reporter continues, "Have the leads helped the case so far?"

"Sometimes," comments Detective Ryan, "they lead to deadends; sometimes they lead to other clues. Therefore, if anyone has any information regarding Mr. Carter's case, please call the South End precinct. Information that may seem insignificant may lead to a suspect."

"How is the family holding up?"

"Well, I think they are standing strong and united. All right, Ms. Lark, that's all the information I have for you today," says Detective Ryan as he turns to enter the precinct.

"We have just heard from Detective Ryan regarding Larry Carter's hit and run case. If anyone has information regarding this case, please call Detective Ryan at (877) 628-2527. This is Carolyn Lark reporting from the South End."

"Mom, I'm sure you have met that Detective Ryan. Why didn't you tell me he was so hot?"

"Laila, I have to get back to work. Since you are here, make yourself useful. Give this paperwork to Erica and this folder to Karen." Brooklin listens to her messages and returns phone calls.

The detective visits Larry at Memorial Hospital after saying good-bye to Brooklin and a brief stop at the precinct. He plans to discuss with Larry how he settled his debt with Big Mel and what Larry's connection is to Mr. Griffin. As he gets closer to Larry's room, he notices Larry's son Ron entering the room.

The hallway is empty so the detective is able to get close enough to Larry's room to overhear Larry and Ron's conversation.

Ron is shouting – strange, since his voice rarely goes above a murmur. "I came home and told Mom, I got more hours at

Logan Courtyard. I was so excited and proud to be able to pay some of our bills. Mom didn't care. Like when I was in school, I was a good student; mom would never even look at my grades. She called me names just like she called you names."

"What kind of names, son?" asks Larry.

"You know what kind of names. The same names she calls you. She hates me because I'm your son and because I look like you. I hate me too."

"Ron, don't say that and your mother doesn't hate you."

"How would you know, you were never there? I loved you, Dad. You were supposed to protect me, to love me. But no, you were too busy running after other women or gambling. And mom, all she wants to do is lay around all day and night getting drunk and hating me because I remind her of you. No matter what I do, she criticizes me. I can never do anything right. I tried to be the best son. But nobody noticed or loved me. It doesn't matter that I help at home and I'm the one who takes care of mom. She's never grateful. Mom won't take care of herself or even keep a job."

"Ron, I know your mother will not work."

Ron's voice grows even louder. "Don't you say anything negative about Mom. This is your fault. She wasn't a drunk until she discovered you were sleeping with anything that wore a dress. You and mom abandoned me."

The detective moves a little closer to the door and checks the hallway again, but no one is in sight. He thinks of the listening device he planted in Larry's room. He knew something was wrong in that family and thought it was reasonable to suspect that Larry would talk to someone sooner or later.

Larry says, "Son, is that the reason you tried to run over me with a car and then drove away leaving me lying in the street? You could have killed me."

"Yes, I drove that car into you. I wanted to get rid of the person who has caused my pain and mom's pain. I thought maybe if you were gone, mom might finally stop hating me."

Then Ron breaks down and cries. Larry tries to comfort him - "Son, don't cry. I forgive you. I know you've had a difficult life."

Outside in the hall, Detective Ryan calls the precinct for back-up and enters Larry's room. Larry and Ron look at him with horror. They realize he has heard everything. Ron weeps, visibly traumatized. The detective stands beside the table near Larry's bed, reaches his hand behind the table and removes the listening device, placing it in his back pocket. "Larry, how long have you known it was your son who drove the car that hit you?"

"I don't know what you're talking about," Larry says with an unsteady voice.

"It's too late now," the detective says. "You and Ron need to come clean and tell the truth. I have solid evidence."

"It's your word against ours," says Larry. Clearly, neither Larry nor Ron saw the detective remove the bug.

Detective Ryan walks over to Ron as two police officers enter the room; he arrests Ron, reads him his rights and handcuffs him. "Ron Carter, do you understand your rights?" Ron nods his head, yes. "Ron, where is the car you were driving when you hit your father?" the detective asks.

"Don't answer anything, son." Larry says.

Detective Ryan points to Ron and tells the officers, "Get him out of here."

Larry calls out to Ron, "I'll call your mother. Don't say anything until you get a lawyer."

Detective Ryan looks at Larry and says, "He's gonna need one."

Chapter 22

Brooklin is working on the computer after spending the afternoon with Greg and a couple of hours with Laila when her cell phone rings. It's Colin.

"Hi, Brooklin, I'm calling to give you an update. The sweep at home for recording devices is completed. None were found."

"Oh thanks, Colin. That's a relief."

"Brooklin, I also have a gift for you. I'll keep it with me until our family dinner on Sunday."

"Colin, a gift? I really cannot accept a gift from you."

"You will *want* this one."

"No, Colin, I don't want a gift."

"Brooklin, I have a puppy for you."

"What? A puppy? Colin, you didn't."

"I did. You and the kids always wanted a dog and I always said no. With you being home alone and not allowing me to return, I think a puppy will be a good companion for you."

"Colin, really? I can't wait to see him. What kind of puppy?"

"Just what you wanted. A Rough Collie. He's a rescue puppy, so he has all his shots and he's neutered."

"What color is he?"

"He's sable and white. I'm going to keep him at the Teen Center with me until Sunday. I'm sure the kids are going to love him too."

"I'll be working at the Teen Center on Friday," says Brooklin, "So I'll see him then."

"I have a list of dog walkers. And included on the list are Luke and Laila," says Colin.

Brooklin laughs. "Sunday, we'll name him. I can't wait for the kids to see him. Thanks, Colin. I'll see you Friday."

"You're welcome, Brooklin. Have a good night ALONE."

Colin smiles when he hears Brooklin's laughter as their call ends. He says to himself, "I want Brooklin out of that hotel and away from that detective. She's my wife and I'm going to take back what belongs to me."

Detective Ryan returns to the precinct to question Ron, who is sitting at the table with his head down. The detective places a recorder on the table, turns it on and sits across from him. "Ron, I want you to tell me about the hit and run." Ron is slouching and fidgeting. "Apparently, you don't understand how much trouble you are in. I can draw a picture, but trust me you may not like it. Now, tell me what happened." Ron's demeanor is somber, and his body language reveals a person who is withdrawn and has given up. "You are still not answering. We already have enough to convict you. If you want to help yourself, you better give me the details."

"My dad told me not to talk until my lawyer arrives."

"Okay, Ron, we can throw you into a cell. Who knows when your mother will sober up enough to call a lawyer?" Ron looks alarmed. "Where is the car?"

"I don't know. I left it on the side of the road somewhere on McCormick Highway."

"What kind of car were you driving that night?"

"A blue Mazda 626. I'm not sure what year – it's an older car."

"Where did you get the car?"

"I found it on McCormick Highway, out of gas. I walked to the store, got gas and took the car."

"Our investigators checked. There was no Mazda reported stolen or missing." Ron looks restless. "How did you get the car started?"

"The keys were under the mat."

"You are telling me, you found a car on the side of the road and the keys were left under the mat?" Ron nods, yes. "Ron, why am I getting the feeling that you're not being completely honest with me? Ron, tell me the truth regarding what happened on the night of the hit and run."

"I got in an argument with my mother. She was yelling and saying things like I was no good and I'm just like my father, no good. When she's drinking, she always brings up dad. I told her I'd be working more hours, but she just kept yelling at me and told me to get out. I didn't try to reason with her because, when I try to convey my feelings, it makes things worse. So I left, since she seemed more upset than usual. After I found the car, I drove down Bauknight Ferry."

"Where were you going? Were you

going to your Dad's house?"

"No, I was just driving when I saw dad get out of his car, I just snapped. I started having flashbacks. I began remembering and hearing mom and everybody's insults and all the pain of being bullied and being called names in school. I don't know. I just lost it. It was as though I couldn't control myself, like my body was acting while my mind was disconnected from what was happening."

"You didn't drive down Bauknight Ferry looking for your father because you were angry and wanted to pay him back for all the hurt you were feeling?"

"No. I didn't even think about being on Bauknight Ferry."

"Ron, that's hard to believe."

"In the hospital, I told my father I hit him intentionally, but I didn't. I just said that to hurt him. All I ever wanted was for my parents to love me and be proud of me. Our family wasn't normal like other families. I've been searching for my identity for as long as I can remember. I don't fit in anywhere. I don't know who I am and what I do know about me, I hate." Ron breaks down and sobs. "I can't believe this. Why me? I didn't ask to be born in this disaster of a life and now look at the mess I'm in. I have never been in trouble. I don't understand how I got here, in this situation. I don't know what to do. I don't know how to fix it."

"Ron, there is no excuse for what you did. Why didn't you ask someone for help? Someone at school?"

"I asked my mother for help. I told her what was going on at school. She didn't care. I was alone, lonely and totally discounted. I've always been alone and had to take care of myself." Ron sniffles, holding back tears. "My mother and father should have cared, but they didn't. They didn't care. No one cared. No one came to my rescue." Ron sobs. "If you don't have family, you don't have anything. I had family and I still didn't have anything."

Detective Ryan turns off the recorder and says to the cop standing at the door, "Take him and book him. Then, allow him to make his phone call." Detective Ryan whispers to the officer, "Place him in Cell One and put him under suicide watch. Make sure no one is placed in the cell with him." After Ron is escorted out of the interrogation room, the detective sits in the room for a few minutes, "Something is not right here. Something is missing."

Detective Ryan returns to the hospital to talk to Larry. He still needs some information from him. When he enters Larry's room, he hears Larry and his brother Mark discussing Ron. They stop talking and stare at him with cold, bitter eyes. "Mark," the detective says and nods in his direction and then immediately shifts his attention to Larry, the person who has caused this havoc. "Larry, I have a few more questions for you."

"I'm not answering any of your questions, Detective."

Detective Ryan looks at Mark and says, "I would like to speak to Larry alone."

"Mark, you don't have to leave," Larry says. "I have nothing to say to Detective Ryan. The detective is the person who needs to leave."

"Larry," Mark says, "I have to contact a lawyer and try to make arrangements to get Ron released. I'll be back after making the provisions for Ron."

The detective turns to Larry and says, "Larry, I spoke to Big Mel and he tells me you settled your debt with him. I'd like to know how you settled your debt?"

"What is your problem, detective? You just arrested my son and you think I'm going to talk to you."

"Larry, I think you and your family are the ones with a problem. Ron is facing a felony conviction."

"That may be; however, I'm not going to answer your questions."

"Oh, you will answer my questions if you want a deal for your son. We can choose to help Ron or not to help."

Larry asks, "What do you want to know?"

"How you settled your debt with Big Mel?"

"If I answer that, I'm admitting to a crime," says Larry.

"If you don't answer, I will have to leak to the streets that you talked. And I think Big Mel will be very unhappy with you. I don't know, but I figure you don't want to be involved in another accident or maybe, even more dire circumstances."

Larry looks frightened. "I'm going to tell you, but can we make some type of deal?"

"I don't know, Larry. You need to start talking right now."

"I bugged Brooklin's office for Big Mel. I didn't want to do it, but I didn't have a choice."

The detective is shocked by Larry's confession, but continues.

"Why did Big Mel want Ms. Covington's office bugged?"

"I don't know," says Larry. "He didn't tell me. I just did what he told me."

"When did you bug her office?"

"I don't know the date. Big Mel supplied the equipment and I bugged her office early one morning, maybe a few weeks before my accident."

"Does anyone else know about this?"

"No, just Big Mel."

"Anyone at the hotel?" the detective asks.

"No, no one at the hotel," says Larry.

Detective Ryan thinks for a minute, trying to decipher all Larry has said. Then he asks, "You were blackmailing Taylor for money?"

"Can I take the fifth?"

"Answer, Larry," the detective says.

"Yes, but the money was Taylor's idea. I was hoping for something different but I accepted the money."

"What were you hoping for?" the detective asks.

Larry laughs and says, "I was hoping to sleep with her. Have you seen that body of hers?"

Detective Ryan interrupts him and asks, "When, where and how much were you paid?"

"I think Taylor gave me $1,000 at the hotel on the day of my accident."

"Larry, what do you know about a Jack Griffin at Griffin Development?"

"Nothing, I've heard of the company, but I don't know any Jack Griffin."

"Are you certain? You haven't heard anyone mention his name?" the detective asks.

"Mention his name?" Larry hesitates, "No, like I said, I've heard of the company, but not Jack Griffin."

"Larry, if you know something, you need to tell me right now."

"I don't know anything about a Jack Griffin," Larry exclaims.

"Okay, Larry, that's all for now. If you remember anything, call me at this number," the detective says as he gives him his card.

"You will help Ron?" asks Larry.

"Let's not get ahead of ourselves. I need to verify the information you gave me." Detective Ryan leaves Larry's hospital room thinking, "That bastard belongs in jail and I'm going to put him there."

Chapter 23

The next morning, Brooklin telephones Jill to finally schedule interviews for a replacement for Taylor. Detective Ryan enters her office as she completes the call. "Hi, Greg. How are you?"

"Tired, I had a long night. I stopped at the restaurant for a cup of coffee for me and tea for you. Brooklin, let's take a walk down to the terraced garden. I have some news about Larry's hit and run case."

Brooklin looks at him a little confused. "News, what type of news? Did you solve the case?"

"Brooklin, let's take that walk. I think the privacy of the terraced garden is what is needed for this conversation." They exit the office and walk down to the terraced garden with coffee and tea in hand.

"Greg, you are making me nervous. What is happening with Larry's case?"

The detective says in a low tone of voice, "Ron was arrested for driving the car that hit Larry and leaving the scene of the crime."

"What? No, Greg, there has to be a

mistake."

"Brooklin, we will talk more when we reach the privacy of the terraced garden."

They continue to walk in silence. They reach the garden, look around to make certain they're alone, and sit at the black wrought iron table near the door. "Now, Greg, what is this all about?"

The detective shares with Brooklin the details of Ron's arrest, and that this information will be released to the media in a couple of hours.

Brooklin is shaken. "Unbelievable, Greg, I wish the outcome could have been different. Things end up the way you least expect."

"I know, Ron is part of the system now."

""This is heartbreaking," she says, her voice shaking.

"Well, his Uncle Mark retained a lawyer and Ron probably will make bail sometime today." The detective doesn't share with Brooklin that he has requested that the DA not release Ron on bail. He would like to monitor and keep Ron under surveillance. "Ron spiraled downward quickly in the hospital and during the interrogation. From what Ron told me about the night of the hit and run, it was like Ron went through some type of psychotic episode -- having no emotional connection to what was happening. I don't think he was in total control of what he was doing."

"Greg, he needs help. His parents failed him," pleads Brooklin.

"I just feel there is more," contends the detective. "Something I'm missing."

"Do you think he's hiding something? Did you find the car?"

"No, and I'm not sure he's being completely honest. No one reported a missing Mazda 626. We checked the computer files. It's a piece of the missing puzzle."

"Greg, I know he's guilty, but can you try to get him into a boot camp with a mental health facility? Maybe they can prescribe some type of anti-depression pills. With counseling, hopefully he can begin rebuilding his life. After so many years of abuse and neglect, Ron deserves to get the help he so desperately needs."

"His lawyer is contesting the confession and said Ron will be changing his plea to 'not guilty.' However, I heard him confess to Larry and I have the confession on tape. Just between you and me, I placed a recording device in Larry's hospital room."

"You bugged Larry's room? Is it legal for a detective to plant a bug?"

The detective ignores the question and replies, "That's the essence of good police work."

"We never learned who planted the bug in my office," proclaims Brooklin.

"Well, I did last night. It was Larry."

"Larry? Why would Larry plant a bug in my office?" she asks.

"To repay a gambling debt to Big Mel."

"I'm confused," says Brooklin. "Big Mel? Why would Big Mel want to plant a bug in my office?"

"I'm pretty certain Big Mel works for Jack Griffin," the detective answers.

Brooklin begins to understand the connection and tells Greg of Jack Griffin's visit to her office.

"I was planning to return to the precinct tomorrow, but now I'm staying here at the hotel."

"No, you are not. I appreciate you

wanting to help, but your job here is done."

"Brooklin."

"No, Greg, I'm serious. I will deal with this myself. However, I would like you to handle arresting Larry for bugging my office."

"Don't worry about that Brooklin, that's a given. I taped Larry and my hospital conversation and I'm going to take pleasure in escorting him out of the hospital and into a jail cell."

"However back to this situation with Jack Griffin …" Brooklin interrupts him.

"Greg, I don't want to lean too much on anyone," Brooklin stresses as she begins to examine the entire situation … so, the bugging didn't have anything to do with the FBI's case … or could there still be some type of connection? "Greg, there may be occasions when I may need to call on you for information, but that will be all. Okay, Greg?"

"Okay, Brooklin," Detective Ryan answers as he leans back in the wrought iron chair. "But if you need me, you know where to reach me." Silently, he thinks to himself, "Jack Griffin, I'm going to take you down." The detective decides to inform Brooklin about one more piece of police business. "There is something I need to tell you and I'm hoping you won't be angry. I assigned a few officers to you after I found the bug in your office."

"You did what?" Brooklin exclaims.

"I had officers assigned to you to make certain you remain safe. However, I gave them specific instructions that they were not to enter the hotel or your home. They just followed your car and kept a close watch when you were alone."

"Greg, were the officers driving a black Dodge?"

"Yes, a black Dodge Charger," he says.

"Okay, Greg, I'm not angry, I'm furious with you. Why didn't you tell me?"

"I thought if you knew, you would not permit the officers to complete their assignment. I wanted to make certain you were safe."

"I realized I was being followed. I just didn't know by whom. I wished you would have told me they were police officers. I appreciate your concern, but can you discontinue this surveillance now that you know Larry planted the bug?"

"Well, I'd like to continue for a few more weeks being that Big Mel and Jack Griffin are interested in Logan Courtyard."

"Greg, pull the officers off of the surveillance duties, please."

"Brooklin, let's just agree to disagree for a moment. Larry's case has been a long and tough road, but we got through it. My reward at the end of this bumpy road is meeting you. I really care for you, Brooklin, and I want you to be safe. Now that I'm returning to the precinct, I won't be at Logan Courtyard every day. With your permission, I would like to see you occasionally, maybe take you to dinner."

"Greg," Brooklin says, "I've enjoyed this time with you and I did let down my guard. But I'm not sure of the next step. I have to admit, I'm attracted to you," she says looking directly into his eyes. "However, I did take vows and I take them seriously. So right now, I just need some time to really think about the situation I find myself in. I also need to concentrate and focus on the new additions to the hotel, opening the theater and the new courtyard."

"Well, you are not ruling out a

relationship with me completely."

"No, maybe. Let's just see what happens."

"Would you mind if I stop in to see you at some point?" asks the detective.

"No, I don't mind. I've come to regard you as a good friend."

"No, Brooklin, don't use the friend card."

She laughs and says, "Just, call first."

Detective Ryan stands to leave and says, "Right, baby steps."

She looks at him and smiles, knowing she is really going to miss this detective.

Back at her desk, Brooklin considers all that has happened when the phone begins ringing. "Hi, Brooklin, its Levy. I want to update you on that project we discussed."

"Yes, what did you learn?" she asks.

"Well, we are continuing to acquire information on the subject, and everything will be included in the report. However, we've learned his assistant resigned and I'm told this lady has a lot of inside information."

"Levy," Brooklin replies, "Place her on the payroll. We can decide in what capacity and time span at a later date. However, we need the inside track. Great work, Levy."

"I thought you might want to grab her as soon as possible. It is my understanding that she is a great worker and was a valued employee."

"Levy, please have a background investigation done and call me with the results. Thanks, Levy, I appreciate this."

"You're welcome, Brooklin, and we are still gathering information."

"Good, tell Jill hello for me." Erica reminds Brooklin that she's expected at a meeting. Brooklin stands, grabs her iPad and forces herself to focus on the meeting.

Back in the office, she returns phone calls, the last one to Colin. "Hi, Colin, I'm returning your call."

"Hi, Brooklin, how are you?"

"I'm okay," she says and brings him up-to-date on Larry's hit and run case.

"Brooklin, that is awful and just tragic for everyone involved."

"It is," she says and they are silent for a moment.

"Brooklin, I know just the thing to cheer you up. Can I come over to the house and cook you dinner? You can have a glass of wine while I massage your feet after dinner."

"No, Colin, I'm going to shower and go to bed early. It's been a very stressful day."

"Brooklin, I love and miss you. No one knows me like you do. You know exactly what I need."

"Apparently not, Colin, you left me."

He pleads with her, "Just think about allowing me to return. Our family deserves a second chance."

"Colin, I just can't talk about this now. I'm running on empty. I will see you and the puppy tomorrow."

"Brooklin are you … will you be home or at the hotel?"

"Colin, I'm going to spend the night at home alone."

He takes a deep breath. "I have another question for you, Brooklin. Is it too late? Brooklin, do you still love me?"

She hesitates, "Yes, Colin, I still love you. Now, good night!"

"Good night, my love. I can wait until you are ready to return to me. I just needed to know that you still love me."

Brooklin tells Erica that she'll be out of the office for about an hour. She drives to the hospital, stands for a moment at the door and gathers her thoughts. Larry is watching television and is shocked when she enters his room. "Brooklin," he mutters.

She looks at him with disgust and says, "You planted a bug in my office?" Larry looks at her and then turns away. "Larry, how could you? I trusted you. Even when I heard all the despicable things people were saying about you, I continued to pay you a salary. Well, I guess, no good deed goes unpunished."

"Brooklin, I'm sorry. I didn't have a choice if I wanted to live or save both legs."

"Do you know why Big Mel wanted my office bugged?" She thinks to herself, "I need to know if this is any way connected to the FBI and if there is a link between the FBI and Jack Griffin." She's becoming very distrustful. She looks at Larry and focuses on him again. "Larry?"

"No, he didn't tell me and I didn't ask."

"I don't know how you live with yourself. Look at how many lives you have affected negatively, all those women, your ex-wife and most of all, your son Ron. It's absolutely nauseating. I'm convinced it's because you are simply irresponsible and do not give a thought to anyone other than yourself. Are you even sorry about the destruction you have caused?"

"Brooklin, I am sorry, truly sorry."

"Yes, you are. You are a sorry excuse for a man. And my heart goes out to Ron, deserted by both parents. Feeling unloved by the very people who the world tells you should love you."

"Brooklin, I didn't know. I didn't know Ron was in such a bad place."

"Really, Larry? You didn't know or you chose to ignore? Larry, you didn't notice that he was yearning for his parents' love? That he hoped there was something he could do that would make a difference? Larry, you and Carmen abandoned your parental responsibility and discarded Ron as though he was useless."

"Brooklin, you're not telling me anything I don't already know."

"Well, fix it. Do the right thing, the courageous thing. Step outside of yourself and help your son."

"I don't know how to," Larry utters.

"How about start with telling your son

that you love him and will stand by him. Let him know that you will be there to offer him emotional support, stability and whatever he needs. Stop the cycle before it gets worse and demonstrate to Ron a healthier way of living. He's lost. Love him back to being."

"I will, I will stand by my son. I know I've been a miserable father to Ron. Brooklin, I want to apologize again for what I did to you. And I want to warn you again, be careful."

Brooklin is exasperated. "You care to tell me what I should be careful of? You want to point me in the right direction?" There's silence. "That's what I thought," and she turns and walks out the door. She stands outside of Larry's room for a minute, anger churning inside. She calls Meghan in accounting, tells her to issue Larry his final paycheck and to enclose a letter notifying him he is terminated. She wants that letter on her desk tomorrow morning for her signature.

Brooklin returns to the hotel to interview the candidates applying for Taylor's position. Levy is present during the interviews and they are impressed with one candidate's computer skills and hotel management experience. Brooklin tells Walt if all goes well with his background check, they will extend an offer to him later this evening. After Walt exits, Levy presents Brooklin with the file on Jack Griffin. They are grateful to Geneva, Jack's former assistant for her help in obtaining information from Jack's computer. Brooklin examines the documents from the investigation and some photos acquired from Griffin's computer. She is stunned as she recognizes a girl in one of the photos. Now Brooklin has another score to settle with Jack. Revenge is not pretty, but it is a great motivator. Brooklin tells Levy, they must determine how to employ this data to obtain the ultimate outcome.

Brooklin works until around 6. Unable to focus on work any longer and not ready to go home, she telephones Jill. Brooklin tells her about the interviews and that she possibly will make an offer to Walt later this evening. Jill asks Brooklin to help her find a dress for a co-workers engagement party. About thirty minutes later, they enter Luhl's Department Store, where style-conscious shoppers can find high quality fashion labels. Luhl's is situated in Hill's fashion district, which houses top designers' shops and boutiques. Jill selects several dresses and enters the dressing room. Brooklin chooses only one and quickly steps to the mirror. After a few minutes, Jill walks out and says, "I don't think I like the color of this dress." Brooklin agrees.

"What do you think about this dress?" Brooklin asks.

"I don't like the way it fits you," Jill says. Are you wearing underwear?"

"Yes, why?"

"Well, you can see the lines under that dress."

"Jill, do you ever go pantyless?"

"I don't wear panties. I go 'Commando.' I let my body breathe."

"Last week, I forgot to pack panties when I stayed a couple nights at Logan Courtyard. At first, I felt uncomfortable, but it was also liberating, freeing."

"It really is," Jill says. "Just like you right now, Brooklin, not restricted or confined." Brooklin thinks about what Jill said, smiles and then returns to the dressing room. After trying on about ten dresses, Jill

purchases two and Brooklin buys one.
"Ready for dinner?" Jill asks.

"Sure" and they walk down the lively pedestrian zone to HerMenia restaurant.

Jill orders a steak and Brooklin orders grilled salmon. "Brooklin, I heard about Ron's arrest on the news. I can't believe Ron hit his own father."

"I know Ron committed this appalling crime. But my heart goes out to him. Ron had a sad and troubled childhood. And now, we're looking at the results."

"Well, we can't choose our family. Does he have anyone supporting him now?"

"He has an uncle and Detective Ryan is talking to the district attorney to try to have Ron remanded in a boot camp that has mental health counselors."

"Well, hopefully, he'll receive help to turn his life around. This will affect his future either negatively or positively. Let's hope for the latter."

"That's true, Jill. If he doesn't receive counseling, the pain he carries can spread to those he comes in contact with and others could be hurt. Often people who are hurting, hurt others," Brooklin says.

"And then people wonder how things like this happen. I talked to Ron a couple of times at the hotel. He seemed okay. I guess he hides his feelings well."

"The teen years are difficult," adds Brooklin, "You're trying to find your way, feeling awkward and struggling to fit in. People don't realize what begins in hallways as joking can transform into unhealthy baggage later."

"Brooklin, this is really upsetting to me."

"It really is. I wish people would think beyond themselves. People need to realize that their words and conduct can cause lifetime scars."

"I know," says Jill, "Including adults who can sometime prey on the vulnerable or bully others as well. Remember the athlete who was tormenting his team mate and the woman who thought her name calling was harmless and used racial comments? Using hurtful words is not blameless. People know what is appropriate and inappropriate. It doesn't matter where you live or your age. Name calling, tormenting, intimidating others are offensive and it hurts."

"I think I will talk to Colin about having the kids at the Teen Center plan a campaign against bullying and include an anti-bullying television commercial in the crusade. Maybe, it will make a difference."

"Brooklin, that's a great idea. If it keeps even one person from being bullied, it will be worth the effort."

"I'm glad Larry survived the hit and run."

"Oh, Brooklin, it would have been awful if Larry had been killed."

"I think after everything has settled," Brooklin says, "I will visit Ron. He's still in lock-up at the precinct because he didn't get bail."

"Brooklin, speaking of the precinct, what's going on with you and the detective?" Brooklin talks about their lunch and outing to the shooting range. "Brooklin, you went to the shooting range? Okay, now I know you really like this man."

"I'm going to own it! I really like this man. However, I'm going to step away from Colin and Greg. I'm going to put my personal life on hold and focus on renewing my commitment to myself."

"I like that, Brooklin, renewal or a rebirth."

"What about you, Jill? What's going on with you?" asks Brooklin.

"Well speaking of starting fresh, I want a new and larger house. I think it's time. Levy and I don't have any children, so what else do we have to spend our money on?   I talked to Levy about a new house last year and he told me, 'Let's wait until next year.' Well, it's next year! I moved into Levy's home when we got married ten years ago. Well now, I want my own house."

"Well, that's understandable," says Brooklin. "Have you been looking?"

"No, I need to bring up the subject with Levy again. Then, I'll contact a realtor. And this time, I will not accept Levy's wavering. I'll keep you informed."

When Jill mentions realtor, Brooklin thinks of Jack Griffin. She decides to only disclose to Jill that Jack Griffin is trying to intimidate her into selling Logan Courtyard and that she has enlisted Levy's help. "I'm not going to let anyone bully me into selling my hotel. I'm tired of people expecting me to give up what I have worked so hard to build."

Jill replies, "Sounds like you may be including Colin in that mix."

Brooklin quickly responds, "Colin asked me if I still love him and I said yes. However, I'm not sure I am still 'in' love with Colin." The waitress interrupts their conversation and asks if they would like dessert, coffee or tea. Jill orders a slice of apple pie and coffee and looks at Brooklin, daring her to comment. Brooklin laughs and orders a cup of tea.

"Brooklin, Colin really hurt you."

"Jill, sometimes when we enter into a relationship, it's not just with other people; it's with ourself as well. The relationship can help us continue to grow or it can stifle us. I gave myself fully to my marriage and children. Now, my children have their own lives and I'm just a consultant. It took some time; however, I finally found a new purpose.

"Brooklin, I'm observing the transformation in you as it's unfolding. You're taking back your power in all aspects of your life. Maybe Colin wants you to allow him to return and help him work through whatever he's going through?"

"That's exactly part of what's wrong

with us. Colin needs to figure out what's going on with him and fix it, like I'm doing."

"Brooklin, you are right. We can't fix other people. Colin has to fix Colin or the cycle will continue."

"Colin and I have to live with our decisions. In an effort to reconcile with me, I think Colin is telling me what he thinks I want to hear." Brooklin smiles and says, "A friend recently told me, he doesn't speculate, he follows the evidence. Well, I'm going to take my time and follow the evidence. I'm choosing to be alone as I regard my situation and I am determined not to settle."

"Brooklin, I just want you to know that Levy and I have your back."

Brooklin smiles at her best friend, "I have your back too, girlfriend. Call me when you're ready to begin looking for that new house. We can look first, narrow your choices down to a few, and then you and Levy can decide on your new home. Have you given any thought to where you'd like to live? I remember you mentioned a few months ago you would like to live closer to the city."

Chapter 24

Jack Griffin walks to the front desk and asks to see Ms. Covington. After checking Brooklin's calendar, Erica walks to the front desk to greet Mr. Griffin. "Hello, Mr. Griffin. I'm sorry Ms. Covington doesn't have any openings today."

"I only need to speak with her for a few minutes."

"I'm sorry, Mr. Griffin, would you like me to schedule an appointment for another day?"

"I do not. Just tell Ms. Covington that Jack Griffin was here to see her."

Brooklin is at home getting ready for work and happy that she hired Walt to replace Taylor as her assistant. She and Levy met with Walt last evening and determined he was perfect for the position. Brooklin walks in her closet and decides to wear the white fitted dress she purchased yesterday with Jill. She looks in the mirror and notices her underwear is visible under the dress. "Should I go commando or wear a thong?" she asks herself. "Normally, I only wear a thong as part of my evening attire. However, it's a new day." She looks in the mirror again, the visible panty lines are literally nonexistent and, as Colin would say, it's a more alluring version of self. She tells herself to make it a habit to shop more often with Jill and maybe even try a little hair color. Convincingly, she says to her image in the mirror, "I have to step out of my comfort zone and start living again. After all, I'm free to do as I please and be whoever I want!

Brooklin arrives at Logan Courtyard, checks in with Erica and takes her quick hotel walk. Today will be another demanding day filled with meetings. She thinks of her dear friend Lydia and reminds herself that she has to stop running from the past and learn from it. "Things happen in life, we get through them," she tells herself as she walks in the direction of the restaurant. "I am where I am today because of my past. I am feeling …"

Suddenly, Jack Griffin appears in front of her. He's leaving the restaurant as she's walking past the entrance. "Ms. Covington, I would like to approach you again regarding selling Logan Courtyard. Are you certain I can't convince you to sell?" Brooklin says nothing. "I made you a generous offer. My advice to you is to take it."

"Mr. Griffin," Brooklin says, "What part of 'I do not want to sell my hotel' do you not understand? Neither you nor your business partner will secure my hotel and certainly not by this ridiculous technique of manipulation. There is no victim here, Mr. Griffin, that you can twist or bend to get whatever you want, but a woman prepared to fight for what is hers."

"Ms. Covington, …" Jack Griffin tries to interrupt her, however Brooklin continues.

"This hotel might seem like an insignificant effort to you. It's not. It's my passion. It has opened the door to my future and restored meaning to my life. You see, I believe one cannot fail unless one quits. And I will not quit on my future. Failure is not an option. So for the last time, Mr. Griffin, I will not sell Logan Courtyard. " She studies this repulsive, corrupt man's face and sees the hardness waiver, doing wonders for her morale. She pulls her shoulders back, lifts her chin and walks away.

Jack Griffin shouts, "Remember, I tried to come to an agreement with you. But no, you want to stand firm. Well, there's no turning back now. Good-bye, Ms. Covington. I'm sure we will meet again." Jack Griffin watches as Brooklin walks down the hall, head held high. Then he observes a man walking toward her. They engage in an intense conversation. Griffin continues to watch them carefully until they disappear around the corner. He knows this man. Where has he seen him before?

Brooklin returns to her office after her discussions first with Jack Griffin and then with Agent Dalton in the hallway. Agent Dalton informed Brooklin that one of the agents in Suite 1107 will be replaced with another agent in the next few hours due to a family emergency. He explained that he checked with the two agents a few minutes earlier in the suite and believes it should be a smooth transition.

A few minutes later, Brooklin and Erica attend meeting after meeting. Erica orders lunch from the restaurant for everyone attending the mid-day conference and they return to the office around 2pm. Brooklin returns phone calls and at 3:15pm, Erica walks in. "Erica, I thought you had left for the day. You told me you were leaving early."

"I am, but I had some work I needed to finish," says Erica. "Brooklin, I never leave without letting you know."

"Erica, if I haven't told you lately, I really appreciate the work you do here."

"Thanks, Brooklin. I absolutely love working at Logan Courtyard and for you. Brooklin, I came to tell you what I overheard when I went to my car earlier. I thought you should know. Mr. Griffin was on his cell and I heard him say: 'Yes, Ms. Covington just needs a little convincing. She hasn't faced the harsh reality. She may just have to learn the hard way. But don't worry--I guarantee she will sell Logan Courtyard. A little birdy just revealed to me how we can kill two birds with one stone. My plan is already in motion.' Then, he got in his car and I didn't hear the rest of the conversation. But, Brooklin, the way he spoke and the tone he used, I think he's dangerous."

"Erica, did he see you or realize you heard him?"

"No, I lowered myself in my car until he drove away."

"Erica listen, don't worry about Jack

Griffin. He will not get his filthy hands on Logan Courtyard. I realize he and his associates practice dirty tactics, but I'm going to play the game better than he does. Knowledge is power," she says to Erica. Brooklin thinks about Griffin showing his hand, identifying Logan Courtyard as his target. "Thanks, Griffin," she says to herself, "now, I will operate from a stronger position and not be blindsided. I hope you and your partners underestimate me and continue to think of me as just a weak, naïve woman. But the game has changed. You were chasing me and now, the tables have turned. It's the only way to deal with bullies, especially those who deem themselves powerful which makes for a sweeter victory. Don't blink an eye, Jack Griffin, because you will fail to see innocent Brooklin bringing down the ceiling to collapse around you. I'm going to make your life miserable. You'll be so busy cleaning up the debris, you won't have an opportunity to focus on Logan Courtyard. Yes, you will attack, but I will launch some missiles of my own."

"Brooklin, where did you go?" interrupts Erica.

"Oh, I was just thinking of some trash I need to shred."

Shortly after, Brooklin walks to her car thinking about a conversation she had with Luke in Memorial's emergency room. She realizes she was wrong. "Sometimes, criminals have a way of inserting themselves into your life. I'm involved with these goons through no fault of my own," she thinks as she phones Luke to remind him of an early morning appointment at the hotel tomorrow. "Of course, he doesn't pick up his phone," Brooklin says sarcastically as she leaves him a message.

At his apartment, Luke hears his phone but ignores it and places it on the tray with the fruit, low-fat yogurt, whole wheat bagel and the bottled waters. He thinks to himself, "Well, it's not a Logan Courtyard breakfast, but it will suffice." He walks back in his bedroom with a smile on his face. Hearing singing coming from the shower, he takes off his boxers and walks into the bathroom. Her back is facing the glass shower door. He looks at her body and thinks how very hot she is. He opens the shower door and asks, "Can

I join you, Taylor?" Taylor grabs Luke and pulls him in the shower.

When Taylor and Luke return to the bedroom, Taylor eyes the breakfast tray and asks, "Luke, where's the coffee?"

"If my baby wants coffee, she will get coffee," Luke says kissing her.

Taylor watches as Luke leaves to get coffee. After eating a few strawberries, she reaches in her pocketbook for her phone. "Hello, Jack."

He immediately asks, "So, how did everything go?"

"Good," says Taylor.

"Can you trust him?"

"Oooh yes! He'll do whatever I ask."

"How can you be certain?" asks Jack.

"Listen, when I call, he comes. The last time I called him, he was at my apartment in less than thirty minutes. This is after being in the emergency room with an injury. He also lied to Detective Ryan to provide me with an alibi. I got him wrapped … Jack, I'm at his apartment and I hear him at the door returning with our coffee. Gotta go."

"All right, Taylor, keep up the good work and get as much information from him as possible. Remember, I don't want him to tell his mother the two of you are together again. With any luck, she will *not* realize where the leak is in her organization. I'll see you tomorrow in the office. Welcome to Griffin Development."

Brooklin begins her drive to the Teen Center to meet her new rough collie after yet another grueling day. She exhales and breathes in the fresh air and says aloud, "There's no turning back now. You want a war, Jack Griffin? You got one!" Her phone rings and she realizes it's Agent Dalton.

"Ms. Covington, a problem has developed and I need you to return to Logan Courtyard as soon as possible."

"What type of problem?" she asks.

"Ms. Covington, we need you to return to the hotel."

"What type of problem?" she repeats.

"Our subject was beaten and left for dead."

Shocked, Brooklin navigates to the side of the road and asks, "What? How did that happen?"

"We are evaluating the crime scene

now."

Brooklin repeats his words slowly, "You're evaluating the crime scene now? Agent Dalton, are you now referring to Suite 1107 in my hotel as a crime scene?" He doesn't respond for a moment, hesitating.

"Ms. Covington, it is imperative that you do not speak to anyone about this occurrence. We would like the perpetrator to believe that the subject is deceased."

"Do you have any idea who committed this assault?" asks Brooklin.

"Well," and he pauses. "Hold for just a minute, Ms. Covington," says Agent Dalton. Then he says to someone in the room, "Yes, let's move forward."

Brooklin hears a man in the background, "Okay, let's go pick up Jack Griffin for questioning."

Mr. Dalton returns to the telephone, "Ms. Covington, our agents are going to pick up a suspect for questioning. We think the man whom our witness was going to testify against is behind this assault. We have learned that the individual who replaced one of our agents at Logan Courtyard was in fact, *not* an FBI agent. He replaced one agent and relieved the second agent to get some rest. When the actual FBI agent arrived, the deed had been done and the impersonator had fled the scene. We're still unsure how the whereabouts of our witness was learned. However, Ms. Covington, when you arrive at Logan Courtyard we can continue our conversation. I do not want to go into too many details over the telephone."

"I hope you're able to gather enough conclusive proof to put this guy away for a long time." Brooklin comments not letting Agent Dalton know she heard that Jack Griffin is the suspect he is referring to.

"At this time, we do not have enough evidence to hold him. He will have his lawyer present during questioning and, therefore, probably will be released. But, we are working the case and evaluating the scene. And, of course, we will have the testimony of our witness. I think we will be able to charge our suspect soon. However, I wish we had something we could hold him on, to keep him in custody until we compile all the evidence against him." says Agent Dalton.

"Well, I will be there shortly," Brooklin says. She severs the connection with Agent Dalton and phones Levy, asking him to meet her at Logan Courtyard immediately and to tell Walt to release the photos we obtained from Griffin's computer to the FBI and media blog in the manner we discussed previously.

Brooklin takes a moment and stares at her reflection in the mirror. She thinks about the events that led her to this place and time. She has worked relentlessly to build the status of and to protect the reputation of Logan Courtyard. Yet, a man has been left for dead in her hotel. She says to herself, "Brooklin, you may have walked into this fiasco with your eyes wide open. However, defeat will not be part of the outcome." Agent Dalton assured her that this will be an undercover investigation and he would do his best to keep Logan Courtyard's name out of the press as much as possible. Yet, she is disturbed that her dispute with Jack Griffin may have had something to do with Mr. Reed's attack. "Jack Griffin, you will not get away with this."

Brooklin circumnavigates back onto the highway making her return to Logan Courtyard thinking how she has intervened and provided a blog gift for the FBI. Sometimes you have to think like a criminal to catch one. "I believe the photos in the media blog will provide the FBI with just what they need to keep Jack Griffin in custody. Good luck, Jack, explaining to the FBI about the pictures of you, your associates and your prostitutes at one of your parties. Especially, you, Jack, who appears to be doing inappropriate things to an underage girl, Kim--whose whereabouts, incidentally, will be inconspicuously leaked to Agent Dalton. When Levy brought the pictures and other information obtained from Jack Griffin's computer to my attention, I immediately recognized Kim, one of the kids from the Teen Center. Jack, how could you? Well, Kim and her family are safe and in counseling. Although Jack, I think you will be very busy providing explanations to the FBI, press and your associates. Oh and let's not forget your wife. Whereas, I gave instructions to obscure the faces of everyone in the photos except yours, Jack, I do believe your associates will still recognize themselves with prostitutes. I can imagine their outrage that these photos are appearing in the media blog with the caption, 'Recognize anyone in these photos? Stay tuned!' How very careless of you, Jack, to leave those pictures on your computer. I'm sure you will immediately delete photos, information and change your passwords. However, we have those photos and considerably more information on your dealings now thanks to your assistant, Geneva, who provided us with the information to infiltrate your computer. And in return, Levy's friend in Miami provided Geneva with a job. Therefore, Jack, you probably will not be suspicious of Geneva being that she has moved on. And undoubtedly, you possibly will not have very much time to focus on Logan Courtyard either. I really think you may have your hands full and I do believe those distinguished colleagues of yours may become a little distrustful of you, Jack."

Brooklin thinks about her decision to hire Walt to replace Taylor. "I really like him and his resume is amazing. Among Walt's many talents is his expertise in the computer field, which will be downplayed at the hotel due to the anonymity relating to the blog. Walt actually has Jack's blog photos originating from a computer in Jack's home state of New Jersey. I'm sure he probably has many adversaries there as well. This should cast a reasonable doubt in Jack's mind regarding my guilt in this matter."

Brooklin drives into her parking space near the front of Logan Courtyard. Since Erica left early today, no one will be inquisitive about her return to the hotel. As Brooklin closes her car door, she is fully aware that there is no turning back now. She's finally on her own. No one is going to decide her future but her. She knows there will always be something drawing her back to Logan Courtyard. She just has to be ready to deal with what is sure to come.

Chapter 25

Ron enters the visitors' room, sits at a table and picks up the telephone. His visitor is sitting at the table across from him, and they stare at each other through the large plexiglass panel separating them. He watches as she picks up the phone. "Ron, why did you want to see me?"

"I've been talking to Detective Ryan and I decided he's right. I'm not going to take all the blame for dad's hit and run. You used me. You never loved me. You continually told me how I should hate dad. You were shouting all those horrible things in the car that night and you said, 'Hit him, hit him, hit him, Ron.' I couldn't think with all the things mom had said and with you shouting at me, I just lost it and then, Erica, you grabbed the wheel. And within an instant, the car hit dad."

"Ron, have you mentioned me or my involvement to anyone?"

"No, but I will tell Detective Ryan right after this visit. You have some guilt in this nightmare, too."

"Ron, listen to me. I came here today to tell you, I am pregnant."

"You're pregnant?"

"Yes, I am going to have your baby. You have an opportunity to be a better parent to your child than your parents were to you. Now, I'm asking you to not tell Detective Ryan or anyone about our relationship or that I was in the car with you that night. He will place me in jail too. You don't want your child to be without his mother and father, do you?"

"No, I don't."

"Well, don't say anything, Ron. I think your sentence will be light. When you get out of jail, we can be a family."

"Erica, I can't believe I'm going to be a father. And, I will be a good father. No one was there for me. But, I will be there for my child." Earlier and painful memories return to Ron's thoughts … "My child will not know the feeling of having someone in the room and feeling totally isolated and like you don't matter … Or believing that you are not worthy of someone caring about you." Ron looks at Erica and says, "I've felt broken all of my life and I don't want my child to have those feelings. So, Erica, you're right. I don't want the mother of my child in jail. You take care of yourself and I will be a model prisoner. I am determined to get out of here as soon as possible to be with the two of you."

"That's good, Ron, and I'll ask Brooklin to give you a job at Logan Courtyard when you're released. I won't come to see you again because I don't want anyone to become suspicious. But, I'll be waiting for you when you get out."

"Okay, Erica, I love you."

"I love you too, Ron" whispers Erica as she hangs up the phone, walks out the door and doesn't look back.

Erica gets in her car and says, "Good-bye Ron, you served your purpose. And Larry, that's payback. I was hoping to rid the world of a bastard like you. However I'm sad to say, it didn't end up that way. You never loved me and I never loved your son. You used me and when I became pregnant, you abandoned me. You had the audacity to offer me money for an abortion. I didn't get the abortion, but I lost our baby anyway. The doctors say high levels of CRH from stress were found which probably caused the miscarriage. Stress from you, Larry. Well, you took my son from me and I took yours from you. Yes, the doctors said it was a boy. I will never see my child, but, Larry, at least you can visit yours in prison." Smiling, Erica thinks back to when she traveled to her mother's home in Delaware to have her blue Mazda 626 repaired and painted dark gray. A few months ago, her mother discussed having her car painted gray. Erica plans to tell her that she had the car painted for her birthday. Totally pleased with herself, she says, "Now, I can remove the repairs to the Mazda from my 'to do' list. Only two other details remain, then I can put this entire ordeal behind me. First, arranging for my mother to trade her Mazda for a new car and second, I must return to speed dating. I need to get pregnant." She daydreams for a few minutes about a new pregnancy. "This time, I think a girl would be nice."

www.ingramcontent.com/pod-product-compliance
Lightning Source LLC
Chambersburg PA
CBHW070050120726
47909CB00002B/339